THE CRIME BANDWAGON

An Eternal Encounter

BY
Amiritha Varshini

pencil

ISBN 978-93-5438-293-2

Published in India 2020 by Pencil

A brand of
One Point Six Technologies Pvt. Ltd.
123, Building J2, Shram Seva Premises,
Wadala Truck Terminal, Wadala (E)
Mumbai 400037, Maharashtra, INDIA
E connect@thepencilapp.com
W www.thepencilapp.com

DISCLAIMER: This is a work of fiction. Names, characters, places, events and incidents are the products of the author's imagination. The opinions expressed in this book do not seek to reflect the views of the Publisher.

AUTHOR BIOGRAPHY

Amiritha Varshini S alias Bhavanthikha, a girl around nineteen can usually be found reading a book. And that book will be more likely a psychological thriller or romance comedy. Writing a novel was always on her bucket list. And eventually it became her everlasting dream. She loves to write poems on love and moon.

Her first book *" Chapter's on my dairy"* is a contempory romantic short story. "T *he Crime Bandwagon"* is her second novel, a psycological thriller and a perfect page-turner.

She is pursuing her engineering degree, B.Tech IT. An engineer by profession and writer by passion!

 She loves cooking, knits very badly, enjoys riding around her town, and otherwise spends far too much time at the computer. She lives in India, with her parents and little sister.   Amiritha Varshini S

CONTENTS

FOREWORD

Copyright © 2020 by Amiritha Varshini S,

Thank You!

Chapter-1

1.1 Brother Saves

Vedha, a young man who is a star co p. He was well- known for his valiant progress. He was residing with his Mom in Mumbai.

That day, he was in his patrol. He was standing opposite to a bank. The street was congested and the honking sounds of the vehicles was clamorous. There was a bank in opposite, a teenager who was dressed in scruffy jeans and baggy T-shirt, the shabby man was trying to open a car's door. Vedha tried to cross the road. But the teenager took a baggage from the car and ran towards the parallel narrow road. Vedha chased him; he ran as fast as a cheetah and grabbed him from his back. He gave a sound thrash, *How dare you manage to steal in this day light?'*   he shouted. The teenager surrendered. Vedha called the constable from his walkie talkie. He obtained the baggage from the man and went near the bank. But the car left. He went to the bank and enquired about the parked car. *'Sir, A teen girl came with a lady in that car. They deposited money and left'* informed the security guard. *'I want to meet the manager'* said Vedha. The security guard took him to manager's cabin. Vedha showed his identity card, *'I'm from police department. I want a customer's detail regarding a robbery case.'* he said and sat opposite to the manager. *'Give us a moment sir. We will help you.'*

said the manager and called the cashier. *'How can I help you sir?'* asked the cashier in a humble tone. Meanwhile, the constable texted the car registration number to Vedha. *'I want the details of the lady who came in this car. Here I have the car's registration number'* said Vedha and handed his phone to them. The cashier and security guard checked the CCTV footage and noticed the teen girl and the lady. They gave the registered address and contact details of the lady. Vedha thanked them and left to his station. He ordered the constable to call and inform about the theft to the lady. He kept the baggage in his car boot.

He continued his duty and left back to home that night. He totally forgot about the baggage in his car. He was busy in his duty and shifts of patrols. Two days later, he opened the boot to get his spare wheel. He saw and recollected about the baggage. He took that inside his home and opened, he saw a bonafide certificate of a girl. She was Anamika, a criminology student. Vedha read the certificate further, he was shocked. His face turned in forlorn. Shamala, Vedha's Mom came, *'Why are you looking tensed?'* she asked. Vedha remained silent. She sat near him and held his hand. *'What happened to you?'* she asked in a calm voice. Vedha led the certificate to her, *'See the date of birth'* he said. His Mom was also shocked. *'This girl is born on the same day when Vedika was born.'* she said with an excitement. *'Yah Mom, you're correct. Vedika w ill be twenty if she was alive'* he said in dismay. *'Past is past. Just f orget about that nightmare'* said his Mom. She took him for sleep and calmed him.

Next day, he went to the station and enquired to the constable about that lady. *'I informed her sir. She declined. She said she did not lose any of her baggage'* replied the constable. *'Okay'* replied Vedha. That day he was looking so intense and was thinking about something. He went to Anamika's college. He headed towards the office room, *'I want see Anamika from Criminology department'* he said. *'May I know, who are you? In what way you belong to her?'* she asked. *'I' m from police department. I want to inquire her.'* he said.

'*Sure sir. We will call her*' said the office lady. Vedha was waiting in the hall. After few minutes, a girl came with the security. She was nervous and frightened. '*This is Anamika sir*' said the security. '*Thank you for bringing her. You can leave now.*' said Vedha. '*How are you Anamika?*' asked Vedha. '*I'm fine sir*' she stammered and was sweating out. '*Come, we will sit under the fan. You're so exhausted.*' said Vedha. '*Sure sir*' she said with a stammered low voice. '*I'm working as an Inspector. I came here to give your belonging.*' he said and gave her baggage. Anamika's face brightened. '*Thank you sir! I was searching for this. I did not know where I misplaced*' she said excitedly. '*You did not misplace it. Last week, a man stole it from your car near the bank.*' he said. '*Yes sir. I came to the bank with my neighbour. Thank you for reaching me. I would have come to collect it, if you have called.*' she said. '*It is my pleasure, Anamika. What made you to choose criminology?* h e asked. '*I love to investigate the truth hidden behind great crimes. Every time, I will be curious to know why the event occurred. That love led me to choose criminology.*' she replied with a pleasure. '*Great. All the best for your career. Here is my visiting card. Do contact me when needed. I will surely help you.*' he said. '*Thank you*' she replied humbly and kept the visiting card in her bag. Rudra dismissed.

A week passed, Vedha received a call, ' *Sir, We are calling from City hospital. A teen girl has met with an accident. We cannot find her contact details. We saw your visiting card in her bag. Please come here to help her.*' he said. '*What is her name?*' asked Vedha. '*We don't know any o t her details about her sir.*' said the man. '*Okay. I will be there within an hour*' said Vedha. Vedha went to the hospital and inquired about the girl to the doctor. The doctor said that the girl had heavy blood loss. Vedha saw the girl from the glass door, he was shocked. It was Anamika. '*Please arrange for AB negative blood. Ask help from family friends and colleagues. This blood group is currently not available in our blood bank.*' informed the doctor. '*Sir, I can donate. I'm AB negative*' said Vedha. '*Great. Do you consume* alcohol?' asked the doctor. *'No sir. I'm a teetotaller.'* said Vedha. The nurse took Vedha to the room where Anamika was kept. They collected his blood through a trip bottle and injected to Anamika. *'She will be fine. Don't worry'* said the doctor. Vedha got permission from his work and asked his Mom to come to the hospital.

Hours went, It was evening, Anamika opened her eyes slowly. She groaned in pain. Vedha and his Mom went near her, *'You are alright my dear.'* said Shamala . *'Where am I now?'* she asked in a tired tone. *'You met with an accident. You are now admitted in the hospital.'* replied Shamala . *'How to inform your family members?'* asked Vedha. Anamika gave her grandfather's contact. After some moments, the old man came rushing. *'Don't worry sir, Anamika is safe.'* said Vedha. *'What happened to her? I was trying to call her from morning, she was not reachable'* he asked anxiously. *'She met with an accident. Now she is fine.'* said Vedha. *'Thank you sir, You helped my girl.'* said the old man holding Vedha's hands. Vedha went to Anamika, but she was sleeping. *'Okay sir, we are leaving. Call me anytime if you need any help.'* said Vedha. The old man again thanked him. Vedha and Shamala left to home.

Vedha felt a strange connection with Anamika. He became nervous when he saw her hurt. He rushed to help her. He felt the feel of her sister in Anamika. He slept happily that day.

1.2 A abrupt bond

Few days passed, Vedha got a phone call, 'Sir, I'm Anamika.' *she said.* 'How are you, Anamika?' *asked Vedha.* 'I'm better now sir.' *she said.* 'Good. Be careful while riding vehicles' *said Vedha.* 'I'm really grateful, I got to know that you donated blood for me.' *thanked Anamika.* 'It is my pleasure, Anamika. You can contact me in any situation, I will surely come to help you.' *said Vedha. Vedha's speech made Anamika to think about the reason behind his unconditional care. Few weeks passed, Anamika was discharged to her home. Vedha invited Anamika and her grandfather to their house warming function.*

It was the day of the function, Anamika and her grandfather left to Vedha's new home. Vedha's Mom welcomed them humbly. 'How are you my dear?' *asked Shamala.* 'I'm fine ma.' *replied Anamika. After few hours, t he function ended happily and the crowd left. Anamika noticed a girl's photo in the wall.* 'Who is she?' *asked Anamika pointing her hands towards the photo.* 'She is my younger daughter, Vedika. She met with an accident and passed away before some years' *said Shamala. Anamika felt sad,* ' Don't worry ma. I'm t here for you.' *she consoled. Mom smiled.* 'Come let's have food together. Call your Grandpa' *said Mom and went to the kitchen. Anamika followed their voice and headed to the backyard. Vedha and grandpa was sitting in the chair and was discussing on something. Anamika noticed an adult giant German Shepherd sitting near Vedha's foot. '* Bose! Bose!' *she called her grandpa. The remained same, they were talking continuously. Anamika stood there, and dialled Vedha.* 'Sir! Mom is calling you both for lunch.' *she said.* ' We are in the backyard. Where are you? Why are you making a call?' *he asked.* 'Sir! I'm standing near the pillar, look at me. I'm really scared of dogs.' *she said in fear.* 'Don't get scared dear. He is my brother. He is well trained. Come here!' *he said with a laugh.* ' No! I'm scared' *she stammered. Vedha got up and brought the dog near Anamika.* 'Caesar stay' *he said. The dog stood still.* 'He is a star detective. He helped us in several cases.' *he said with a smile and tapped on Caesar's head. Anamika's heart beat fast,* 'Just tou c h him ' *he said.* 'Caesar! Shake hands' *said Vedha and the dog raised his paw. Anamika held his paw. She smiled.* 'Sir! Mom is calling us to have food.' *she said.   Vedha smiled,* 'Don't call me sir. It is not good to hear.' *said Vedha with a smile.* 'Okay, Mr Policeman' *replied Anamika with a giggle. All three   headed to the dine and got seated and Mom served them.* 'Where is Anamika's parents. I've never seen them.' *asked Mom. Anamika's face shrunk.* 'At her age of three,

Anamika's mother passed away. Her father had no mercy; he left Anamika and moved abroad. Later he married a lady and now he is well settled. I am her maternal grandfather. Later me and my wife brought up Anamika.' *replied her grandpa in a sad voice. Mom hugged her,* 'See now, you've got a mother and a brother. We are there for you, Anamika.' *calmed Mom. Vedha held Anamika's hand,* 'Losses are very painful, but the pain is not permanent.' *said Vedha. Anamika smiled.* 'I lost my sister at my age ten. She was four years younger to me. My world revolved around her. One day, We went on a tour in the vacation. We did not know that day will end up in trag edy . A truck lost it's control and dashed us. Our car was crashed and turned topsy turvy. My little sister was stuck under the car. My father' s legs got locked in the wheel. Later we were taken to hospital. My sister passed away, treatments went useless. My dad's right leg was amputated. Later, he los t his job. He became a drunkard, he couldn't accept his daughter's loss. After a year, my dad passed away because of heart attack.' *said Vedha. His face turned red and his eyes poured out tears. Anamika held his hand warmly.* 'I was a little boy who lost h is beloved sister and dearest father. Our family shattered. Years went, we were living our life. This recent days were a lucky period of my life, I met you. A girl who was born on the same day when my little sister was born. Destiny brought y ou to me. I somehow feel my little sister in y ou .' *said Vedha. Anamika hugged Vedha in happy tears.* 'I'm your brother. You're my little sister. I will destroy anything that harm you.' *promised Vedha. The moments were filled with pure love and promises.*

After some time, Anamika and her grandpa left to their home. Anamika's life changed with Vedha's abrupt unconditional bond. She felt the showering fortune.

Chapter-2

2.1 The New visitor

Few months passed, Vedha and Anamika developed a palsy-walsy bond. Everyday Vedha used to drop her in college. Both families spent their weekends together. Life was moving merrily, they spent best times together. Soon, Vedha was promoted as Deputy commissioner of police. H e was transf err ed to Pune. He worked as fire, he was trapping major crimes, he became a sensational cop of that time. Meanwhile, Anamika joined in her post graduation and was also preparing for Union Public Service Commission examinations. She started a YouTube channel and spoke about crimes occurring in the country. She gained popularity and became a social media influencer. She was seen as gallant women. Vedha and Anamika did not meet for months; their conversation was only through phone call. *'Bhaiya, when will you come here? I badly miss you'* wretched Anamika. *'Guddu, you r brother is the deputy commissioner. The city really needs his service'* said Vedha with a laugh. *'So funny, come here for a couple of days, Mom is really worried about you'* she pleaded. *'Okay fine, I will try to come soon '* consoled Vedha. *'That's a good boy'* said Anamika with a funny gesture. *'Concentrate and prepare for your exams. You're always busy in uploading your videos in YouTube.'* warned Vedha. *'Hey bro, don't be so funny. I have huge fan base.'* she replied with a proud filled laugh. *'Hey! don't be playful'* he warned in a high voice.

'Okay... Okay... Cool.. I'm studying. Don't worry.' she calmed him. 'Good' he replied with a smile. ' I'll *talk to you tomorrow*' he said and ended the call.

After a week, Vedha arrived to Mumbai. Anamika arranged for a beano. The car honked outside the gate, Vedha got down from the car. Anamika ran to receive her brother. There was a stone in the pathway; she toppled near Vedha's foot. *'You no need to seek my blessings. My blessings are always there for you.'* said Vedha with a huge laugh and raised Anamika. Anamika stared at him, her eyes squeezed. *'Vedha, Don't pull her legs. She was flying to meet you.'* said Shamala . *'Ma, I did not pull her legs. She fell by herself.'* he replied with a giggle. Shamala took him inside and the party was started . The y all had great time. The house turned into a delightful paradise . Vedha left to Pune that night. He came to Mumbai for a day to visit all of them.

It was late that night, Anamika and her grandpa walked in the silent roads leading to their home. *' Mr. Bose! Can you get me an ice-cream?'* asked Anamika. *'Ana! No'* replied Bose. A man with thick beard, dressed in black came out of the old villa which was abandoned for many years. Anamika rushed behind her grandpa. *'What are you doing, Anamika?'* scolded B ose . The man gave a weird look on her. *'Sir, A man was waitin g for a long time, he said to give this parcel to you'* said the bearded man and gave the parcel. *'Thank You!'* said grandpa and looked at the address in the parcel. *'Oh! It was my colleague. Anyway thanks... Who are you?'* questioned grandpa. *'I'm Rudra. I'm the new tenant of this villa.'* he said with a smile. *' I'm Bose, your neighbour.'* replied grandpa. Anamika interrupted, *'Oh my god! Be careful in this villa. It is deserted for many years. This place is really creepy; it is an abode of bats. I think there is something paranormal. I don't think it is safe for you...'* she said with funny gestures. Grandpa closed her mouth, *'Better shut your mouth, Anamika'* he raged. *'Sorry sir, She is a playful girl.'* apologised Bose. *'Never mind'* he replied with a smile. Anamika's face was full of weird gestures. *'Goodnight Mr Bose ! Nice meeting you'* said Rudra and headed towards the villa. There were two adult Rottweiler dogs; he tied them near the inner iron gate. *'Dada! This man is looking weird.'* said Anamika seriously. *'Stay quiet, Let's go home'* said grandpa. Anamika and Bose returned back to their home.

2.2 Blooming in heart

It was a usual morning; Bose was sitting before the television and was watching morning news. Anamika took her cup of coffee and went to the balcony. She noticed black smoke from the nearby building. Screams of people was echoing. 'Dada! Dada!' *she shouted.* 'Dada! Are you deaf? Just come here and see what is happening?' *again she shouted.* 'Ana! Wait. I'm coming' *he said and rushed to her.* 'I think a kind of fire accident. Let's go down and see.' *he said and both went to the spot. People gathered in the road. The fire flares where spreading.* 'Did anyone inform to ambulance?' *asked grandpa to a man.* 'These old chaps are only fit for asking questions. Useless!' *said the man. Grandpa's face turned sad.* 'Oh man! You are a hero, why are you standing here? Go and save the people who are stuck inside.' *said Anamika to the man in sarcasm. The man stared at her.* 'Ana! Be quiet, Let's go from here' *said grandpa and took her away. They saw a young man helping the people in the building. He carried few kids and left them out from the fired building. Seeing that, other few young men joined him for help.* 'Dada! Do you remember that guy? We met him yesterday in the haunted Vila.' *she said.* 'Yes! It seems he is a good person' *he said. Anamika was staring at him, forgetting everything.* 'Don't flirt at him' *said Bose with a huge laugh. Anamika turned her face to him,* 'You old man! Talk wisely' *she said.* 'I'm wise enough than you silly girl' *he replied with a laugh.*

That day Rudra looked like a heroic figure to the residents. Anamika ran to her flat and got a jar of water. 'Hi! Have some water' *she said and gave the jar towards him.* 'Thank You!' *replied Rudra with a smile and drank the water.* 'Do you remember me? We actually met yesterday' *she said with stammered voice.* 'I do remember. You were drunken' *he said.* 'Drunken?' *she replied with a shock.* 'Sorry! You literally blabbered' *he replied with a giggle.* 'Excuse me!' *she yelled in rage.* 'Cool... Cool' *he tried to calm her. There was a tap on Anamika's shoulder, It was grandp a.* 'Where did you go?' *he questioned.* 'I came to give water to the se guys' *she said. Grandpa turned over. Rudra,* 'Hi, young man. You're great. You've a good spirit in you to save the people.' *he appreciated.* 'Thank you sir! And sorry Anamika, I did not mean to hurt you. I just said in a funny way.' *said Rudra.* 'Alright!' *she said.* 'But your face is still in downcast' *he said.* 'I'm fine' *she replied.* 'Let's meet some day, Bye!' *he said and ran back to the building.* 'Don't do this peculiar behaviour, Ana! It's not nice, you're grown up' *said Bose.* 'Dada! Stop this! I love the way I am' *she replied.* 'People can't talk to you' *he said and took her home.*

She went to her room and saw her phone, there were 5 missed calls from Vedha. She dialled back. 'Why are you not picking the calls?' *asked Vedha.* 'Bhaiya! A fire accident occurred in the nearby building.' *she said.* 'Okay. Is anyone hurt?' *he enquired.* 'No! A hero saved all of them' *she said.* 'Hero?' *he asked astonishingly.* 'Yes! He is Rudra. He is a smart young man. He saved everyone like a superman' *she said with her eyebrows high. Bose grabbed her phone and asked,* 'Did you reach safe, Vedha? 'Yes Dada! I'm safe. Who is that? Ana is reciting poems about a hero.' *he replied.* 'She is a crazy girl, blabbering all time. There was a fire accident in a building; a young man saved the people in fire. She was speaking about him.' *he replied. Both were on laughs,* 'Where did she go now?' *asked Vedha.* 'She is sitting before the TV, Do you want to talk to her?' *asked Bose.* 'No Dada! I will talk to her later, I've gotta go.' *he replied.*

Chapter-3

3.1 Best Kills

Next day, Anamika moved to w ake up her grandpa who was asleep. Dada! Why are you still sleeping?' *asked Anamika.* 'I'm unable to get up. Feeling tired' *he replied in low voice.* 'Okay! You take rest, I will take care of everything' *she replied.* 'Wait for some time, I will prepare breakfast.' *he said.* 'Hello old man, you can take rest for a while. YouTube will never fail to help this YouTuber. I can manage to cook seeing videos' *she said with her head up. Bose gave a smile,* 'Learn to manage everything. After my departure , no one is there to take care of you' *he said with drops of tears in his eyes.* 'This old man has gone mad.' *she said with a knock in his head.*

Anamika felt sad inside though she was smiling out. The reality killed her happiness. She was an eccedentesiast. She prepared breakfast and took to grandpa's room. 'Here is the breakfast. Don't forget to brush your teeth before you eat.' *she said with a laugh. Dada too laughed.* 'Okay Dada! I'm going to shoot a video for my channel , don't disturb me for some time.' *she said.* 'Okay Madam!' *he replied with a giggle.*

She took the newspaper and went to her room, she read each every bits of news but nothing seemed interesting. In a corner of the newspaper, there was a news " Brave Transgender saves a girl", she felt something intriguing. She read further. The news occurred on the previous day, four men attempted to rape a girl who was returning to her home from work. A transgender lady who went through that way saved the girl and thrashed the men and attacked them brutally with a heavy rock. One man died on the spot and other three were admitted in critical care. The news triggered her. She called Vedha and explained about this case, 'Can you help me to know more about this case?' *she asked.* 'Wait, I will check with my friend in your city.' *he said. After an hour, Vedha called back.* 'Ana! I found. What you said was right. I have something more for you. The transgender lady admitted the girl to the nearby hospital and then escaped.' *he said.* 'Did they enquire the girl about the transgender lady?' *she asked.* 'Yes! She did not remember the lady's face. As she fainted in panic in the spot. She was in a befuddled state' *he replied.* 'This is really strange. Any evidences?' *she asked.* 'So far, No!' *he said.* ' Okay Bhaiya! Thank you. Wait for an awesome video.' *she said and ended the call. She drafted the script for the video and set up the tripod and camera for shoot. She started,* "Transgender! The society has given them a black remark. What comes on your mind after hearing the word transgender?..... Most of the time, It won't be a good thought. The vision of the society has been like this for many years. It has been a stereotype. But today, I read from the news paper . A transgender lady saved a girl from being raped. She thrashed the men and threw a heavy rock on their head. She was seen ferocious in the scene. The girl was in fainted state in the spot. Later the transgender lady admitted the girl in the hospital and escaped from the scene. Who was that lady? Why she was so ferocious in the crime scene? We have no answers for any questions. There is no evidence or clue to find the lady. I see this case as an eye opener to break the traditional visions on them. Everyone should abolish the negative thought on them. They should be praised and raised. Comment your opinions in the comment section below . Subscribe to my channel 'VOICE FOR CHANGE', I will be uploading videos on latest cases in our country. This is Anamika, standing off. Bye! Bye!" *she spoke. Her bold statements and opinions on the affairs gained good audiences.* 'This video is gonna be a massive hit.' *she thought and started to edit the video. After hours of editing, she made a perfect output to be uploaded. She went to grandpa's room; grandpa was her best reviewer of all time. The old man was seen tired o n the bed. She kept her palms in his forehead,* 'Dada! Are you fine?' *she asked.* 'I don't know why, I feel really tired today.' *he replied.* 'Shall we go to hospital?' *she asked.* ' No Ana! I'm unable to move. I'll be fine after some time.' *he replied. Anamika's mind couldn't stop worrying. She called their family doctor to check her Dada. After some time, the doctor came home and checked the old man. He analysed him and said that his blood pressure is very low. He prescribed few medicines.* 'Don't worry Ana! Your Dada will be alright' *said the doctor and left from there. Few hours passed, Anamika was lying on the couch with her arms on her head, her eyes was closed. Grandpa came out of his room and saw her. He judged that she was distressed. He took a glass of water, wetted his fingers and sprinkled the drops on her face. Anamika opened her eyes in shock and stared. Grandpa was laughed at her.* 'Dada! Have you gone mad?' *she asked.* 'Yeah! I've gone mad after seeing this mad lying silently.' *he said with a giggle. Both giggled.* 'Ana! I'll cook masala maggi for you.' *he said. Anamika's face lightened up. Bose went to the kitchen and started cooking, Anamika took her video recorder,* 'Here is my grandpa, he will teach you to cook maggi desi style' *she said with a happy laugh and recorded.* 'Don't do this Ana! Why are you shooting this?' *asked grandpa with his hands closing the camera lens.* 'Let me shoot, I'm gonna post this in Instagram.' *she said with a giggle.* 'Crazy girl!' *he said and continued chopping the vegetables. Grandpa lighted up the pan and sautéd the veggies in hot oil.* 'Dada! Great going, I've streamed live in Instagram. Give a look to the thousand people watching you.' *she exclaimed. Grandpa's face turned red in blush. He sprinkled masala and poured water and dropped the noodles into it.* 'We have drowned the noodles boy in the water, soon he will turn into India's favourite soft noodles. Bye guys! I'm hungry, I'll catch you later' *she said and turned off the live stream. Dada turned and stared at her.* 'Shall I say you something?' *he asked. She nodded her head.* 'Media is great platform. It has both pros and cons. You have a good audience. Do something valid. Why are you streaming these causal stuffs?' *he asked.* 'Dada! I really speak valuable stuffs in my YouTube, I was rewarded with a great response. I'm streaming my casual stuffs just for memories. I will be great when we see after some years. People love to watch lifestyles. This is called video blogging. Don't worry, trust me.' *she said with a smile. Bose smiled.* 'I trust you my girl, have this noodles fast.' *he said. Both had the food and enjoyed chatting leisurely. Hours passed, Anamika made her grandpa to sleep.* 'Oh my god! I totally forgot about the video which I recorded' *she thought and rushed to her room. She hastily, switched the laptop and started to post the video. After an hour of network struggle, she successfully uploaded the video.* 'Sorry for the late post! Like, comment and share this video.' *she pinned in the YouTube comment tab.* 'Ushhhh! You' re becoming an irresponsible girl, Ana!' *she thought and went for sleep. The life of this teen girl was going smoothly, she had a lovable brother, a friendly grandpa, and she was evolving as a good social media influencer.*

3.2 Thank you Man!

A night, it was around two, Grandpa was collapsed on the wash-room floor, he was breathing heavily. *'God!'* he groaned and held his chest. Anamika's scream was echoing. She was restless; she was unable to do anything rather shouting for help. Rudra was relaxing in his balcony; he found something was wrong in Anamika's house. He rushed there and knocked the door. Anamika ran and opened the door, ' *What is happening?'* exclaimed Rudra. ' *Dada! Dada!'* she yelled with a flow of tears, her face was pale, she was trembling in frustration and her hand was pointing at the wash-room. *'Let me see'* he said and ran. Grandpa was lying there unconscious ly . Rudra carried the old man and ran to his car. Anamika locked the door and followed him. They left to the city hospital and admitted grandpa in emergency ward. He was taken to the critical care and the treatment was started. Anamika was sitting in the waiting hall of the hospital , *'D on't worry!, your grandpa will be fine... Now, Call any of your relatives for help, it will be tough for you to manage alone.'* said Rudra. Anamika sat numb, she was staring at a place, Rudra shook her shoulders, *'Are you alright?'* he asked. Anamika fainted. Rudra yelled for help, a nurse came and sprinkled some water on her face. *'She is stunned and weak.'* said the nurse. *'Yes! She is worried about her grandfather.'* said Rudra. *'I'll be fine. Thank you!'* said Anamika in dull voic e. The nurse left from there. *'How is D ada?'* asked Anamika. *'He is healing. Doctor said he is out of danger.'* said Rudra. Anamika was thinking about something deeply. After some time, *'Can I make a call? Can you give your mobile?'* she asked. *'Sure'* he said and gave his mobile. Rudra walked and sat in the chair. Anamika dialled to Vedha, *' Bhaiya! I'm Ana. Dada suffered with chest pain and now he is hospital.'* she said with a weep. *'Hey! What are you saying? How is he now?'* he asked with a shock. *' He is fine. But still in ICU '* she replied. *'Thank god! Mom is in our native or else she would have been with you'* he said. *'Oh! Okay'* she replied. *'Now how are you going to manage?'* he asked. *'I'll manage myself'* she stammered. Vedha was worried. *'Call me if anything'* he said and ended the call. Anamika went to Rudra, *'Thank You!'* she said and returned back his phone. *'Thank you! You helped us in the right time. I don't know what would've happened if you didn't come.'* She said. *'Thank You is needless'* he replied. She smiled. *'You can leave, it is already late. I can manage.'* she said. *' I have no issues. I know you are alone. I know it is difficult for you to manage.'* he said. She smiled. *'I can be here with you, if you wish'* he replied. *'Thank you again!'* she replied. *'Thank You is needless again.'* he replied with a giggle. They both sat again in the sitting space. Few hours passed, Rudra rubbed his stomach, *'Did you have your dinner?'* he asked. Anamika's eyes were sleepy, *'No!'* she replied with a yawn. He nodded his head. *'Shall we go and have something? I'm really hungry'* he said with a pity face. Anamika looked at her wrist watch, *'It is 4 am. How can we find food at this time?'* she asked. *'Don't worry; I know a friend's shop. Food will be served all time.'* he said. *'Okay'* she said. *'Shall we go there?'* he asked. *'Sure'* she replied. Anamika took her handbag. She went to a nurse in the nurse's station, *'Sister! We are going to have food. Take care of Grandpa. If anything, can you call us?'* she asked. *'Don't worry dear; your grandpa is sleeping peacefully. We will call you if any emergency. You can go without worrying.'* replied the nurse. Anamika and Rudra got into the car and started to the restaurant. *'It is quite far, about 10 kilometres'* said Rudra. Anamika nodded her head. *'I will guarantee the taste of the food served in that restaurant.'* he said with a smile. She smiled. Rudra turned on the music. The melody was accompanying their travel. *'So, what is your name?'* he asked. *'Anamika'* she said. *'Sounds good'* he replied with a smile. Their car was going fast in the empty highway road, Anamika's hair was moving in the hair, her hands were holding it. Rudra's eyes were on her, his lips murmuring the lyrics of the melody played. After few minutes, *'What about your family?'* asked Anamika. *'I have my father. He is a patient; he'll be in bed rest. And I have my little brother, he is a challenged kid.'* he said with a painful smile. *'I'm sorry'* she replied. *'No! No worry'* he said . *'What about your parents?'* he asked. *'Both are not with me. My mother passed away, my dad is married to another lady. I have only my grandpa. He is my everything.'* she said. *'Life is hard'* he said. Anamika closed her eyes and sighed. After few minutes, *'We have reached the restaurant.'* said Rudra. They parked the car and entered into the restaurant. *'Hey Rudra! How are you man?'* asked a man with a hug. *'I'm fine Zakir'* he replied. *'Okay, sit fast. What would you like to have?'* he said and moved the chairs for them to sit. *'What is available now?'* he asked. The man listed the food items. Anamika and Rudra got seated. *'Get me parathas and chicken gravy.'* said Ru d ra. *'What would you like to have Anamika?'* asked Rudra. *'Chapati'* she said. Zakir went to the kitchen. The server boy kept a jar of water o n their table. Rudra was surf ing in his mobile, and his legs were vibrating. Anamika was looking around like a lost kid. Few minutes passed, Anamika tried to pour water from the j ug , but spilled some water o n the table, *'Be careful'* said Rudra.

'Oops!' she replied.   *'Zakir! Be fast, we're really hungry.'* yelled Rudra. Anamika laughed. *'Why are you laughing?'* he asked. 'No!' she said and controlled her laugh. Zakir rushed with the food, ' *Sorry for being late'* he said and placed the food items in the table. The food was hot; the steam was coming out from the dish. Rudra tore the paratha into pieces and poured the gravy into it. He loaded the pieces into his mouth. Anamika was controlling her laugh and ha d her chapatis. *'Taste the chapat i s with this gravy'* he said with mouth full of food. Anamika giggle d . ' *You are laughing for this too'* he said with a stare. Anamika smiled. Both had their food peacefully. And t he y moved to the payment counter. Zakir gave the bill. Anamika opened her handbag. Rudra took the wallet from his pocket. *'I will pay'* she said. *'No! No! '* he replied. *'No Rudra! I will pay'* she said again. Zakir was looking at both of them. *'Shall I keep a match for you both and the winner should pay this bill'* he asked with a laugh. Both giggled. Rudra held Anamika's hand, and gave money to Zakir in other hand. *'You can pay on our next outing '* he said with a smile. *'Hmm Hmm'* said Anamika. Both got back in to the car and they headed towards the hospital. Anamika's eyes was drowsy and her head was falling down. After few minutes, she fell asleep. Rudra turned off the music. He was staring at her and he couldn't take his eyes. " *Don't look at her man!"* he said to himself. His face was blossomed. He felt relaxed and happy. After some moments, they reached the hospital. Rudra tapped on Anamika's shoulder, *'We have reached'* he said. Anamika woke up and looked around, *'Oh! We have reached to the hospital'* she said in a tired voice. She tied her hair in bun and walked in tiredly. Rudra followed her. They went to the nurse station and informed that they have reached. They went to sitting space again. *'You are looking so tired'* he said. *'I'm terribly tired, totally exhausted'* she replied. Rudra peered; *'I'll manage to sleep o n this bench'* she said and lied in the metallic bench by covering herself with her dupatta. Rudra sat in the opposite bench and was surfing in his mobile. Anamika closed her eyes slowly. Rudra stared at her, he tried to look away, but he couldn't control his eyes. H e   was smiling without a ny reason. His heart had thousands of butterflies flying inside. He felt like heaven.

It was 6 am, next day ; Anamika woke and searched for Rudra. Anamika walked around to find Rudra. She saw him sleeping in the corner of that hall. Anamika felt pity, s he went and tried to wake him up. *'Rudra! Rudra!'* she called tapping on his shoulders. He opened his eyes and made a long yawn . *'Good morning Anamika'* he said. *'Why are you sleeping here?'* she asked with a saddened face. He laughed, *'I'm not short like you, I can't adjust myself in the bench'* he said with a giggle. *'Don't be crazy.'* she replied. Rudra smiled. *'You can go home. I'll manage. Your father is also a patient and you should take care of your brother'* she said sadly. *'Don't worry; I've called my friend to help them. She'll help them.'* he said with a smile. Days passed on like this, Anamika loved Rudra's accompany.

After a week, grandpa was discharged from the hospital.

Chapter- 4

4.1 Take my Heart!

Grandpa was getting better, but he was not so energetic like before. He needed special care and help. Anamika was the only person to take care of him; this created a great fret in him. Vedha got permission from his duty and visited them with Shamala . Both decided to stay there for a week. Meanwhile, Anamika's last video on YouTube gained huge appreciation. Many other leading channels called her for interviews. *'Dada! They are asking me for interviews, shall I attend?'* she asked. *'This is surprising! You are asking permissions to me.'* he said with a laugh. Anamika stared at him silently. *'Yes Dada, she has turned into an obedient girl.'* said Vedha with a wink. Anamika smiled. *'Yes, she has turned into a nice girl. But I miss that old crazy girl.'* said Bose. Shamala came into the room with a bowl of hot soup, *' Please have this soup. It is totally nutritious.'* she said and kept the big soup bowl on the table. She pulled the chair and sat near the table and transferred the soup in to four cups, Vedha was showing weird reactions. Anamika raised her eyes and asked *'What?'* in whispers. He nodded his head and signed it' ll tastes worst. Anamika giggled. She walked to the balcony, and saw Rudra who was cleaning the car. Anamika waved her hands at him. *'Hey Rudra!'* she yelled with a smiled. He stared at her furiously and went inside his villa . Anamika was clueless about his behaviour. *'He came by himself and helped me, now he is staring at me angrily. Why? What did I do? '* she thought by biting her nails. Vedha followed her to the balcony, *'What are you doing here? '* he asked. *'Nothing'* she stammered. *'Come soon and have that soup'* he said with a huge laugh. She replied *'No'*. *'How can you say this?'* he said and dragged her to Grandpa's room. Anamika burst into laughs. The whole scene turned into a heaven of laughter.

Few days passed, Vedha returned to his city, his permission period was over and he was called for duty. Shamala left back to her home. That day, Anamika was going to the office of a famous YouTube media channel. She chose to travel through a public bus. The bus was vacant, few people were seated here and there. Anamika sat near the window, She was gazing out. All of a sudden, a palm came waving in front of her face. She turned aside, *'Hey Anamika!'* yelled Rudra with a bright smile. Anamika gave a perplexed look. *' How are you?'* he asked. *'Good'* she stammered. *' Why are looking at me like this?'* he questioned. *'Nothing'* she said with a cute smile. *' Where are you going?'* he asked. *' I'm going for an interview'* she replied. *' Yeah, It happens'* he said with a smile. Anamika raised her eyebrows, *'What happens?'* she asked . *'This will ultimately happen for a celebrity.'* he said with a laugh. Anamika smiled and hit his shoulder. After some minutes, *'My stop came. Will see you later.'* she said and got down from the bus. He stared at her with a blush , h e did not understand the reason behind his pleasure. He felt something special when he is with her. Rudra also got down from the running bus, Anamika did not notice him. She walked into the office of that YouTube channel. Rudra was waiting in the cafe which was a djacent to that office. Nearly, after two hours, Rudra noticed Anamika walking out from the office. He followed her silently. Anamika walked few steps ahead and stopped in a tender coconut shop. *'Bhaiya! Give me a tender coconut'* said Anamika. The man in the shop took the cleaver, chopped the top of the coconut and gave it to Anamika. The day was hot and the tender coconut warmed her. *'What you want man?'* yelled the man to

Rudra. *'Can you give me Cappuccino?'* asked Rudra with a laugh. The man stared at him angrily. Anamika turned at Rudra, *'Hey Rudra!'* called Anamika. Rudra raised his hand and waved at her with a smile. *'Give me a tender coconut'* said Rudra to the man with an irritated face. *'These kind of men will not leave a single girl in the street.'* murmured the man and gave the coconut to him. *'How was your interview madam?'* he asked with a smile. *'Yeah, It went great. It will be uploaded by next week'* she replied. *'Great!'* he said. *'How are you here?'* Anamika asked. *'Yeah! I came to meet a friend.'* he said. *'Oh! That's nice'* she said and walked after paying to the man. Rudra pulled the man's hand and placed the cash. Then he ran behind her, *'Where are you going now?'* h e yelled. *'I'm leaving home.'* she said. Rudra nodded his head. *'What about you?'* she asked. *'I am going to my favourite place, my abode of peace'* he said with a charming smile. Anamika smiled, *'Where is that place?'* she asked. *'Hmmm... I can't say you. I can take you.'* he said with wink. *'I would love to join you. Even I'm seeking for peace.'* she said.

Rudra delighted, *'That's my girl'* he said. *'Before leaving, I'll make a call to my grandpa'* she said. *'Sure'* he r eplied with a smile. Anamika called, *'Dada! I'll be late today. So be safe. Make a call if any emergency. I'll inform to secretary uncle that you're alone, so that he'll have a look at you.'* she said over the call. *'Blah... Blah... Enough girl. Carry on'* he said with a laugh and ended the call. *'Done. Shall we move?'* she asked. *'Yeah'* he said. Both walked to the bus stand, *'Can you give me a hint on that place?'* she asked in excitement. *'Nah.... Nah... I hate to break surprises'* he said and raised his eye brows . *'I really hate suspense'* she said with her chins down. Rudra grabbed and shook her cheeks. *'What are you doing?'* she asked a nd gave a confused look . *'Oops.. Sorry'* he said. She nodded and smiled. They got in to the bus.

Few minutes passed, *' When will we reach the place? '* she asked. *'Now'* he said delightfully. Anamika peered and felt excited. *'Yeah! Get down'* he said. Both got down from the bus, *'We have to walk few steps ahead, so follow me.'* he said. *'Okay'* she said and followed him.

They walked in the broad road and there was a big arch, *'SWARGA CHARITY '* read Anamika from the board. He smiled. They walked through the narrow road from the Arch. *'Swarga means heaven. Like it's name, this place is really a heaven. I believe you'll definitely love being here.'* he said. They entered in, a man ran to them, *'Hey Rudra, It is really a surprise seeing you here today.'* he exclaimed. *' How are you uncle?'* he asked and hugged him. *'I'm fine. What about you?'* enquired the man. *'I'm great'* he replied. The man turned at Anamika, *' Who is this?'* he asked. *' She is my friend'* he said with a smile. *'Welcome'* invited the man. The man took him to the hall. *'Uncle, today I'm really happy. Call our children. I will arrange for lunch today.'* said Rudra. The man smiled, *'Oh! Today' s lunch is already provided by someone else.'* he said. *'Okay, I will arrange for dinner'* he said. The man agreed. *'But surely, I want to spend some time with them.'* he said. *'Com e on m an! This is your place.'* he said tapped at his shoulder. *'I'm going to arrange for the meal'* he send and left. Rudra took the chairs, *'Madam, please take your seat.'* he said. A namika smiled and sat. Rudra took his phone and was surfing. Anamika was looking around the photos in the hall. Few minutes passed, bell rang. *'Hey sweetheart! It is time for lunch. I'll go and help them.'* he said. *'I will also help'* she said with a smile. He smiled and took her t o the kitchen.

Rudra carried a big barrel filled with rice. *'Take the pail of curry and follow me.'* he said. Anamika took the pail and followed him. The children were seated in the hall. *'Rudra uncle'* they screamed in happiness. *'Hey dolls.'* he replied They rushed to him, *'The barrel is too hot. Everyone should be seated'* he said. *'Everyone sit, First have our lunch.'* instructed the man. Rudra and Anamika served them. L ater , they sat with the children and played. They were surrounded with little kids, h appiness and laughter w ere bloomed.

It was four, ' *Anamika, before we leave. we'll just go and speak to the people in the adults compartment.'* he said. *'Sure!'* she said with a bright smile. A fter some time , they moved there, *'Hey Rudra has come'* said a granny. P eople over there surrounded them and showed their love. ' *When did you come?'* asked an old man. *'I came here around two. We served lunch to our dolls and now we came here to see you .'* he replied. *'See him! He is not fair nowadays. Just visiting us for name sake.'* s aid a granny. He hugged her and said, *'Never ma! We have less time today. I came here with my friend'.* He introduced Anamika to them. All spoke hearty words and shared pure love. *'Shall we leave, lady?'* he asked. Anamika agreed. The whole people ranging from kids to old ones followed them to the entrance and gave a warm send-off. Both left out and walked in the narrow road. Anamika remained silent. Both looked at each other. After few moments, *'Madam, You did not comment anything about today.'* he said. Anamika smiled, her cheeks turned red. She remained silent. *'Madam'* he said and raised his eyebrows.

Anamika burst into tears, and it was happy tears. *'What happened?'* he stopped and asked her. Anamika turned hugged h im, her eyes dropped out tears . *'Hey Anamika'* called Rudra. *'I love you'* she said. Rudra was stunned, h e went speechless. *'Yes. I love you Rudra. You have a beautiful heart. I want to be with you forever. I want to witness this day forever with you.'* she said. H e remained still in shock. Anamika's face had mixed emotions, her eyes were filled with droplets of tears, her cheeks turned red and her lips carried a pleasant smile. Rudra wiped her tears and hugged closely. The climate cooled and the clouds drizzled. *'You will be forever mine. I love you'* he said. Both left to their homes. The day ended with an unexpected expression of emotions.

4.2 Happy Days

Next day bloomed, it was one. Rudra called Anamika. *'Did you reach home safely?'* he asked. *'Yes'* she replied. *'How is your grandpa?'* he asked. *'He is fine. He has slept now'* she replied. *'Okay'* he said. Both remained silent for some seconds. *'Anamika, Are you sure about our love?'* he asked. *'Yes. I will be sure, if I loved something. I will not be confused on which I love'* she replied. He remained silent. She said, *'You might think, This girl c onfessed her love too soon. She might not be firm...'.* *'Anamika, No'* h e said. *'No Rudra. These thoughts will definitely flood in your mind. You'll be confused. I want to say you one thing, I don't wish to miss great things in my life. I promise, I will never leave you'* she said. *'I never get what I love. Happiness is very short in my life. I love you, I feel something magical when I' m with you. I want to be with you forever. I want to make beautiful memories'* he said. Rudra smiled, he became emotional. *'You have a beautiful heart, I want to own it. We will make it'* she said with a smile. She smiled, *' Good night Rudra. Sleep well'* she said. *' Okay! Before that, come to your balcony. I want to see you.'* he said. *'Okay. Stay in the call'* she said went to the balcony. Rudra came out to his front space, *'Love you'* he said with a flying kiss. *'Love you too'* she replied and ended the call. She curled under her blanke t and blossomed in blush. Few days passed, one morning, Rudra was scrolling his Instagram. Meme pages were flooded with Anamika's trolls. Rudra called her, *'Hey, how are you doing?'* he asked. *' G ood'* she replied in a low and tired voice. *' I sense something is wrong with you. What happened?'* he asked. *'Did you see my last video in my channel? I spoke about caste system. I did not mean anything wrong, I conveyed caste system s lead to many mafias. Now t he netizens are trolling me.'* she replied. *' D ear! You are in a great phase of life. You have a great focus from people. These judgements will not be positive all time. Take your compliments as your motivation. Ignore your negative comments. Just move forward with your work. Sweetheart!'* he replied. She smiled. *'I can do something to change your mood'* he said. *'What?'* she giggled. *'I will take you out.'* he said with smile.

'Wow! It is a master plan.' she replied with a laugh. *'Okay get ready for our date'* he said and ended the call with a smile.

It was five, the sun started to set mildly. Rudra texted Anamika to get ready for outing. Anamika stood in front of the mirror and bloomed in a smile. Bose walked and stood behind her. *'Someone is admiring their own beauty'* he whispered. Anamika stood still. *' Ana! '* he yelled and shook her. *'Dada '* she whined. *' Your behaviour is different nowadays'* he said. *'Why so?'* she asked. *'You are showing som e symptoms of love.'* he replied. Anamika blushed. *'Answer me. Am I right?'* a sked Bose. Anamika smiled, *'Yes, I'm going for my first date. So bless me'* she said went to the door. *'Ayushman Bhava'* replied grandpa with a laugh. Anamika laughed, *'Take care Dada! I'll be back in some time.'* she said and left. She walked to Rudra's villa.

He was cleaning his car, *'H ere you are!'* he yelled. Anamika waved her hand with a smile. *' Please come in.'* he welcomed. Anamika stopped, *'Your dogs'* she said in fright and pointed at his dogs. *'Don't get scared dear. They are tied strong. They will not cause any harm to you.'* he said with a smile. She opened the gate's latch and walked in. She looked around. *'You have totally changed this place. Now it is looking great'* she said with smile. He smiled. *'Is someone inside?'* she asked. Rudra stilled. *'Rudra? '* she called again. *'Who?'* he asked in a low voice. *'Your family? '* she replied. He remained silent. *' Yes!, George and Alan'* he replied and gave a strange look. *' I remember. Your father and brother'* she replied with smile. Rudra b ehaved strange. *'I wish to visit them someday.'* she said. He remained silent. Anamika stared at him. *'Get in the car. We are leaving'* he said and his face had no emotions. Anamika got in his car and they left from t here. Rudra drove the car, he remained silent. Anamika felt something fishy in his behaviour. *" I think their family will not accept our love"* she thought to herself and came to a conclusion.

Where are you taking me, Mr?' she asked. *'Say me dear. Where would you like to go?'* he asked. Anamika felt annoyed , *'You said me that you are taking me out. But now you are asking me to say the place.'* she said. *'Ha..Ha.. This is your problem. Cool down baby!'* he said with a tap in her head. Rudra headed to the Marine Drive. They parked the car and s at on the t read parallel to the se a . The breeze kissed their face, the mild heat of the setting sun was soothing. *'This place's beauty is phenomenal in nights.'* he said and combed his hair with his f ingers. *'Yes!'* she replied. Both sat o n the lane and admired the beauty of the sea and the city's view. Rudra held her hands, *'How a re you feel ing now?'* he asked. *'Safe'* she r eplied with a smile. Rudra rubbed and warmed her hands. *'I'm an orphan. You are the only person for me to call as a relation'* he said. Anamika hugged him. *'One day, you bravely saved the people who were stuck in fire . Other day, you helped me and Dada. Other day, you showed me your people in the charity. You are great man, you have a beautiful heart.'* she said. Rudra smiled. *'I never expected, I'll receive love from such an amazing person.'* she said. *'I too never expected a girl will come and vanquish my lonely days completely.'* he said. The sun set and the scene turned dark. The lights of the city shined like fireflies, the beach's breeze warmed them.

'Shall we have something?' he asked. *'Yeah sure. It is getting late.'* she said. They stood, crossed the road and got into a restaurant. After few minutes a waiter approached them, *' What you like to have Anamika?'* asked Rudra. Anamika read the menu card. *'Better, you do one thing, order for me also. Today, let me have in your favour.'* he said with smile. Anamika smiled. *'One Schezwan fried rice, one set of Kulcha, one set of Naan, One Mexican rice, Kadai veggie gravy'* she listed. Rudra was shocked, *' Have you ordered the food for your whole family? '* he asked in shock. Anamika laughed, *' I have only ordered the main course. We should end with desserts too'* she said with a wink. *'Oh my god!'* he laughed. After few minutes, a group of men entered the restaurant. One from that gang noticed Anamika,

'She is Anamika' he said and pointed at her. *'Is she your Ex?'* replied an other guy in the gang. *'Shut-up man!'* he yelled and walked towards Anamika. *'Ma' am . I'm your big fan. I love your videos and your boldness'* he said. Anamika smile d , *'Thank you'* she replied. *'She is a sanctimonious fake feminist man! Don't run behind her'* said a guy from the gang and laughed hard. Anamika's face s hrunk . Rudra got up from his seat, *'Hey you! Get away from us. Who are you to comment on her?'* he shouted in rage. *'Rudra stay calm'* said Anamika and made him to s it.

' Don't disturb them' yelled the waiter and instructed t he gang to leave away. A transgender lady sitting in the corner table was noticing everything happening there. After few minutes, *'Enjoy the food'* said the waiter and placed the food o n their table. Anamika smiled. Rudra was tensed and his face looked intense , *'Hey man. You should never show your anger to your food. So, now enjoy the aesthetic of this dine'* she said with a bright smile. Rudra s miled. *'You know, I forget everything when I see these Kulcha parathas.'* said Anamika with a smile. Rudra giggl ed. Both started to have their food. *'Woah! This is called the feel heaven man!'* yelled Anamika. *'What?'* asked Rudra. *'Having your favourite delicacies is the real feel of heaven'* she expressed. *' You are a real food lover.'* he said with a smile. *'Yes of course'* she agreed. Both completed the food, *'Now it is time for desserts'* said Anamika. *'No... Anamika. My stomach is full'* he said tired ly . *'No way. You should definitely have. I don't mind if you puke'* she said with a laugh. *'You crazy!'* he replied with a laugh. Anamika called the waiter and ordered two Faloodas. Both completed the dessert and winded up. The y went to the paying counter and asked for the bill. Rudra left his hands in his pocket and tried to take his wallet out. *' This is my turn to pay'* she said and held his hands. He smiled, *'You have a good memory power'* he replied. *'Yes'* she said and paid the bill.

Both headed to the exit door. The transgender lady in the restaurant followed them, *'Anamika!'* she called. Anamika turned towards her. *'Yes Ma' a m'* she replied with a smile. *'God bless you!*

You're really a bold girl. I admire you.' she said. Anamika gave a perplexed look. *'You have spoken about me and my community. I'm the one who saved the girl from the rape.'* she said. Anamika shocked, *' Wow really!'* she screamed in happiness. *'Yes my dear. You have great thoughts. I bless you for a great future.'* she said. *'I'm going speechless. I feel blessed'* she replied happily. The transgender lady smiled and left the spot. Rudra hugged her, *'This is the real reward of your hardwork '* she said with a smile. *'Yes!'* she replied. *'The truth is, I gained a huge respect on you after watching that specific video. You are doing a great work'* he said with a smile. Anamika felt out of the world. *'I always have huge respect on them. Transgender is a gender alike male and female. But the society has covered them with a black blanket.'* she said. *'You're absolutely right.'* he replied. Both returned back to their homes. Anamika felt blessed and happy. Her worst day turned unforgettable.

Chapter- 5

5.1 Mystery and Heart Break

Few days passed, *'Bhaiya! Dada seems to be so tired, he is unable to get up from the bed.'* she cried. *'Ana! Be cool... From when he is behaving like this?'* he asked. *' P assed two days'* she replied. *'Alright! I'll say Mom to help you. Don't worry, we'll do something.'* he calmed her. *'Okay Bhaiya!'* she said. *'Don't get panic'* he calmed him. She calmed. *' And one more thing, I'm may get transferred by this week.'* he said. Anamika laughed, *'Stop being mischievous Bhaiya. This is your sixth transfer.'* she said. Rudra giggled, *'It not because of my mischief, it is because of savagery towards the suspects.'* he replied. *'True! You're a sensational person. I'm always proud to be your sister.'* she said. Rudra smiled. *' You know something!'* she asked. *'What?'* he replied. *'Before meeting you, I read about you in the newspaper. There were days when I used to google about you.'* she said. Rudra smiled, *' Oh really! I too saw you in YouTube. Once, I showed your videos to my colleagues. I liked you because you used the platform of media in the right way '* he said. *'Bhaiya! Enough of self-appraisals .'* she said with a laugh. *' Yeah Ana! You're right. Take care of Dada. Firstly, don't get panic.'* he said and ended the call.

Anamika headed to Grandpa's room, he was in deep sleep. She took the newspaper and left to her room. *" It has been couple of weeks by posting a video in my channel . I should find a proper content now"* she thought to herself. She took a glance on all news pieces, *"BRUTAL MURDERS O N THE CHARITY SECRETARIES'* she read out. She focused deep in that news and noticed the murder occurred in the Swarga Charity. Her heart stopped for a second, she took her phone and dialled Rudra. She rang several times, but he did not pick the calls. She rushed down and went to his villa. She rang the bell and tapped the gate's latch. Nobody turned out. The Rottweilers barked ferociously at her. She got scared and returned back to her flat. She researched more facts about the case, she got to know that the two secretaries were the head of the chain of charities. Lastly, they were seen in the Swarga Charity collecting funds. Later, they left from there and was kidnapped. The suspect had hit them with a hammer and gashed them with a machete all over their body. Their right arms w ere missing. There were few dog bites noticed o n their knees. T he corpses w ere disposed in the sewage. The were no traces and clues of the suspect. She was perplexed, she decided to visit the charity next day and then make a perfect video regarding this case. She was firm not to mislead the fact s of the case. She headed to grandpa's room, she looked at the clock, it was 12 noon. She tapped grandpa, *'Lazy Dada! w ake up fast, it is scorch ing outside and the sun kissing your bald.'* she said. Grandpa remained stilled, *'Dada!'* she yelled and shook him. Her hear t beat fast, she moved her forefinger near his nose, she felt no breath. *'Dada!'* she screamed and fell down. She sobbed hardly. Her phone rang, she moved and attended the call, it was S hamala , *'Hey dear, I've made Dada's favourite Vada Pavs. I'm heading there, I heard he is feeling dozy. These Pavs will make him energetic.'* she said happily. Anamika's eyes poured tears continuously, her face turned red , *'Ma! Dada is no more'* she stammered. *'What?'* cried S hamala . Anamika remained silent and cried hardly. *'Ana! Don't cry. I'm coming there as soon as possible.'* cried Shamala and rushed to Anamika's spot. Anamika lied o n the floor in a benumbed state. Her eyes were dropping out tears and her face turned pale. S hamala went to B ose and checked him, then she called the ambulance. She moved to Anamika and lifted up her up, s he   wiped her tears and gave a tight hug, Anamika cried loudly, *He made me as an orphan.'* she screamed with a loud cry. *'No... No... You should never say this. I'm there for you. Vedha is there.'* s aid Shamala. The ambulance arrived, *'Get up dear! Ambulance has arrived.'* she said. Two men entered and transferred Grandpa's body in the stretcher and placed in the ambulance. Anamika and Shamala followed the ambulance. After reaching hospital, grandpa's body was taken for analysis. *'Ma'am please wait here for a while, our doctor is examining'* said the nurse. Mom called and informed Vedha about Grandpa's death, ' *Give the phone to Ana.'* said Vedha in saddened tone. Mom gave the phone to her, *'Hello Anamika'* called Vedha. Anamika sobbed. Vedha cried and he was unable to console her. Anamika dropped the phone, Shamala consoled and picked the phone. The nurse and the doctor arrived towards them. *'Vedha. We will call you later. Doctor has arrived'* she said and ended the call. *'He is declared dead. Please sign these forms'* he is said and gave the sheets of paper to them. Anamika cried hard and signed the paper. *'Okay Ma'am you can leave now, the body will be send through ambulance to your home.'* he said and left. Both headed to their home.

Grandpa's body was kept in the hall of their home. *'How to inform about this to your relatives?'* asked Mom. *'I'll inform to one of my uncle and we will ask him to inform other s '* she replied. Mom went to the kitchen and prepared tea for Anamika , *'Dear, Have this tea'* s aid Shamala . *'No ma'* she cried. *'You should have the   strength to overcome this pain. So have this'* r eplied Shamala and warmed her. Anamika had the tea and w alked to grandpa's room. She went to his table, touched his stack of books, his spectacles and tablets box. She opened his cupboard and saw a photo stuck there, in that photo Anamika was hugging him. *'Dada!'* she sobbed and fell down. By that time, her maternal uncle's family arrived there. S hamala came and lifted her, *'See, your uncle and family has arrived. Get up dear.'* she said. Anamika moved to the hall. *'Ana!'* they cried and hugged her . She smiled in pain. Meanwhile, her uncle called his relatives and informed about grandpa's dismiss. *'Who is that lady?'* asked her aunt. *'Ma'* she replied. Her aunt gave and perplexed look. *'I'm her friend's Mom'* said S hamala. *'Brother'* she said in a saddened tone. Shamala smiled, *'Okay Ana!, go and lie for a while. '* she said and took her to her room. Anamika slept in few minutes, soon the house was flooded with people who came to offer condolences to Bose. It was around ten, Vedha reached there. He sobbed and offered his condolences to grandpa and rushed to Anamika. *'Hey Vedha! When did you come?'* asked Mom. *'Now'* he replied and saw Anamika. *'She is sleeping'* replied Mom. *'Yeah! Did she have something?'* he asked. *'No! She had a cup of tea long back'* she replied. Vedha tapped her shoulders, *'Ana! Ana!'* he called. Anamika opened her eyes slowly. She saw Vedha, and screamed in agony, *'Bhaiya!'* she sobbed and hugged him. Vedha' s eyes dropped tears, *'Don't cry!'* he said and warmed her. The relatives noticed Vedha and was enquiring about him. People there was unable to understand and accept their bond, 'Brother? How is that possible?' they whispered among themselves. Vedha took her out and they had their dinner. They went on a drive and got relaxed. After an hour, they returned back to home, all the relatives left from there. H er uncle and his family was only there. *'Had dinner?'* asked uncle. Anamika nodded his head and sat near grandpa's box. Mom and her aunt was cleaning the place. Vedha sat on the chair, *'What is his profession?'* asked uncle. *'I'm the Deputy Superintendent of Mumbai'* he replied. *'Oh!'* replied uncle in shock. *'How did you get to know about Anamika?'* enquired uncle. *'It is a long tale'* he replied with a laugh. Uncle smiled, *'What h ave you planned, Ana?'* h e asked. Anamika stared angrily, *' My Dada has brought up me as a brave independent girl. I don't want your concern. My Dada gave me life when you all left me. Throw away your concerns in trash.'* she shouted. Her uncle's face changed, *'Ana! Stop this'* said Vedha. *'She is in frustration. That's why she is talking all this'* said Vedha. Her uncle l eft out in rage. Anamika walked to the balcony, she saw Rudra was sitting out in the rocking-chair at his front space. His face was impassive and he was smoking his cigar and blowing out smoke. Anamika expected his concern, his act disheartened her more. *"Do this man suffer in short-sightedness?"* she thought to returned back to her room sadly.

Next day, Dada's funeral was over and all relatives left. *'This is life. People will question you. They gossip at you. But no one will end up in being there for you.'* said Anamika with a painful smile. She moved and stood near her grandpa's photo. *'Ana! Stop ruining your peace by thinking about such stuffs'* replied Vedha. Anamika smiled. *'Shall I say you something?'* asked S hamala. Anamika nodded. *'Better come with us . I'm also living alone.'* said Mom. Vedha ran to Mom and hugged her. Anamika t hought deeply . *'What are you thinking?'* yelled Vedha in happiness. *'We consider you as our girl. So don't have any hesitation.'* said S hamala and hugged Anamika. Anamika went speechless became emotional. After few days, Anamika vacated her flat and moved to Vedha's home. That night, Vedha ran to Anamika, *' I've got a surprise for you'* he said. *'What?'* she asked excitedly. Vedha gave a cover to her, *'What is this?'* she asked. *'Open it and see'* he replied. Anamika opened and found a letter in the cover, she read it further. *'We are happy to inform that Mr. Vedha is transferred to Mumbai city. We are wishing for his effective service to be continued in the city.'* she screamed in happiness and ran to Mom. *'Ma, see this. Vedha is transferred to Mumbai.'* she yelled. *'Ye s dear'* she replied and fed a sweet to Anamika and Vedha. *'This is a very happy news but I don't know how many days will this last ?'* she said with a laugh. Vedha stared at her, *'Why?'* he questioned. *'You may anytime get wild on your suspects and they are going to to transfer you to other city. So I'm not gonna fly high'* she replied with a laugh. Vedha gave a knock on her head. *'Okay dears. Let's go for sleep. It is already late.'* instructed S hamala.

Anamika was facing a new environment, Mom and Vedha made her feel comfortable.

5.2 Missing Love

Anamika's final year exams arrived, she had one month time preparation. That morning, Anamika took the newspaper and started reading. A bit of news shocked her, " Teen footballer was murdered and was disposed naked in the sewage". She read further, she got to know more, He was kidnapped from a roadhouse. He had several machete cuts all over the body. He was hammered and strangled to death. Later the naked corpse was disposed in the sewage. L eft arm in the corpse was amputated an d missing. This news connected her, she thought deeply and remembered about the murder of the secretaries in Swarga Charity. Anamika ran to Vedha's room, Vedha was sleeping, 'Bhaiya! Bhaiya!' *she shouted.* 'Ana! Give peace for some time.' *he whined.* 'Bhaiya! Get up ' *she yelled and shook him.*

Vedha got up and rubbed his eyes, 'What?' *he yelled.* 'Bhaiya! Read this news about the murder of a f ootballer . The pattern of the kill is similar to another murder which happened few weeks back.' *she said. Vedha read the news further,* 'Give me a minute' *she said and ran to her room and got her diary in which she wrote the contents for her channel.* 'See, In this murder, two secretaries are also murdered similarly. I guess the same suspect is behind t hese murders. The suspect is amputating a n arm from the victim. He/ she is hammering the victims and finally disposing the c orpse in a sewage.' *she said. Vedha thought deeply.* ' Are the bod ies disposed in same sewage?' *he asked.* 'No Bhaiya!' *she replied. Vedha nodded and thought deeply.* 'The secretaries were disposed near Dharavi. And this footballer is disposed near Juhu.' *she informed.* 'He is playing a clever game' *he replied.* 'Bhaiya! Now you are transferred here. You can show more concentration in this case. Or else it may lead to great tension later.' *she said.* 'You're right' *he replied. Vedha understood the seriousness of these consecutive murders, he left to the station and discussed about this to his higher officials.*

Anamika was spending hours of study, 'Dear, have this milk and study.' *said S hamala . Anamika smiled and got the glass of milk.* 'You're having a great understanding and interest in these detective stuffs.' *said S hamala.* 'Yes Ma! This is my ever lasting dream.' *she replied with a smile.* 'You'll reach great highs dear' *exclaimed Shamala.* 'Ma! My friends are calling me for a discussion about our project. Shall I go?' *she asked.* 'Done behave like a kid. Fly free!' *replied Shamala with a smile.*

After few moments, Anamika left to Rudra's villa. She called him over phone, 'Hello Rudra!' *she called.* 'Yeah Ana!' *h e replied.* 'I want to speak to you.' *she said.* 'Sure. Where are you now?' *he asked.* 'I'm standing in front of your home' *she said.* 'Wait! I'm coming down.' *he said and came out. Rudra's look was contrary. His thick beard and moustache was clean shaved. His curly hair was shortened till skin.* 'Hey sweetheart! Where did you disappear?' *he asked.* 'Me?' *she yelled in shock. Rudra hugged her,* ' You know how much I missed you? I came to your flat, but it was v acant ' *he cried. Anamika felt bad,* 'Sorry! My grandpa passed away last week. And I vacated to my brother's house. I was in downcast and frustrat ion. I did not think about anything else.' *she replied despondent ly .* 'Alright! I sensed something was wrong.' *he s aid.* 'Ye p! ' *she replied.* 'Departures are painful. But m oving on is life.' *he e xclaimed with a hug.* ' Rudra, I'm leaving. I bluffed to my Mom and came to meet you ' *she said and got back on her scooter hastily.* 'Okay! Don't forget to make calls and texts ' *he said. Anamika smiled and drove back to her home.*

Few weeks passed, Anamika's final exams and projects got over. Vedha was busy and tensed, he was working day and night. That day, 'Ana! Ana!..... Mom, were is Ana?' *he yelled and entered home.* 'Why are you yelling?' *asked S hamala and called Anamika.* 'Did you read the newspaper yesterday?' *he asked.* 'No Bhaiya! I was busy yesterday.' *she replied.* ' T he same sort of murders occurred again , and this time it was three men. One was 29, other was 32, other was just 18' *he said in dismay.* 'What?' *she replied in shock.* 'Yes.' *he replied.* 'Some prior actions should be taken as soon as possible.' *she replied.* 'I've arranged for a meeting today. I've called all the officials in the department to discuss the importance of this case.'

he said. 'Right' *she replied.* 'I want to say you something.' *he said. She nodded and agreed.* 'I want your active participation. From tomorrow, get ready and come with me.' *he said. Anamika and S hamala gave a shocked reaction.* 'Bhaiya...' *she stammered.*

Ana! Making videos and posting in your social media is not going help you. You are a criminology student. You r analysing skills are immense. So accompany me, you'll learn more.' *he said.* 'You can do it my girl' *said S hamala. Anamika felt excite d,* "I will inform about this to Rudra. He will be really happy" *she thought to herself and called him. But her calls got disconnected.* " Better I will knock his door. He is unavailable in calls." *she thought and left to his spot.* 'Rudra!' *she yelled in happiness and tapped the gate's latch.* "Where are those bully Rottweilers?" *she thought. But the villa seemed deserted. She felt no people w ere inside and noticed the big lock in the inner gate. She was mazed. She also noticed a* "TO-LET" *card-board tied to the window. She dialled to th e phone number mentioned in the card-board ,* 'Hello, Who is this?' *asked a man on other side of the call.* 'I'm a friend o f Rudra . I came to see him but his house is vacant.' *she said.* ' He has vacated from there two days ago.' *he informed.* 'Okay thank you sir!' *she replied and ended the call. Her heart sank, she felt unfair.* "He is not ready to inform me that he is vacating his home. Finally he will blame me." *she thought. She felt distressed and returned back to her home.*

Chapter-6

6.1 The Follow Up

Next day, Anamika got ready in formal attire, she was dressed in white shirt and khaki pant. She styled her hair in pony. Vedha was reading the newspaper with his cup of coffee. Anamika walked out from her room, Vedha turned at her and his cheeks broadened, *'Sassy Anamika!'* he yelled. Anamika smiled and showed peace sign in fingers. She ran to Mom and touched her feet, *'All the best my dear.'* b lessed Shamala. *'Bhaiya! Get ready soon.'* yelled Anamika. Vedha rushed to his room. After some moments, Anamika and Vedha left. *'Don't you feel this get-up is too much?'* he asked with a laugh. *'Our costume matter s, It gives an impression to others and confidence to you'* she replied. *'Agreed!'* he said and gave a tap on her cheeks. *'Where are you taking me? '* she asked. *' Hmm.... Now we' re going to Hanuman Mandir and then to Raju Bhai's store. '* he replied. *'Who is Raju Bhai?'* she asked. *'I will reveal soon'* he replied with a wink. They reached to Hanuman temple and offered their prayers. Then Vedha took Anamika to a fast food stall. *'Welcome sir!'* welcomed the shop-keeper. Both sat on the dining benches, *' Get two Kachodi and two masala tea'* he ordered. *' Sure sir'* replied the shop-keeper and went to prepare their food. *' He is Raju Bhai! I love the food served here.'* he said. Anamika smiled. The shop-keeper placed the ordered food in the table. Anamika had a bit e of kachodi, *' Woah.... It is yummy'* she compl i mented. Rudra smiled,

'Have a sip of this masala tea' he said. Anamika sipped, *'Heavenly'* she exclaimed . After few minutes, they left from there after paying. *' Next?'* she asked. *' We are heading to Swarga Charity'* he replied. *'I've been there before. '* she said. *'When?'* he asked. Anamika stopped for a second, *'Once I visited there with one of my friend'* she replied. *'Cool! W e should enquire about the secretaries there'* he said. *'Yes, right!'* she replied.

They drove to the charity, the narrow road flashed the memories of Rudra in Anamika. She became emotional and her face turned sad. Soon, they walked to the office of the charity. The old man came, *'Who is this?'* he asked. *'I'm Vedha, deputy superintendent of police. We've come to enquire about the death of the secretaries.'* he said. *'Yes sir. the y're the head of our charity.'* he said. *'That is a known factor. Could you say us some more information about them? ..... Do they have any revenge? Something like that'* said Vedha. The man baffled. He remained silent for minutes. *'No sir'* he said. *'Why should you think so much to say no? '*, Vedha raised his voice. The man faltered. *'This is not going to work out.'* said Vedha anxiously. *'Walk to the station'* he yelled. *'Bhaiya! Cool down '* calmed Anamika. *'Sir! Sir!.... There was a small dispute on that day. They are not good. They are wicked.'* the man pleaded. *'Show us the camera footage on the day of the murder.'* said Vedha. The man opened the drawer of the table and took a pile of CDs. He took one of the CD from the pile and inserted to the player, *'Sir, this is footage of that day'* said the man and turned the monitor to Vedha. The footage was played , the secretaries engaged in an argument with the old man. Then, Rudra interpreted, and yelled ferociously. Rudra thrashed the secretaries, and the old man and few other people from the charity held Rudra and stopped him from hitting. *'What is happening here?'* asked Vedha.

Anamika b ecame restless by seeing Rudra in row. The old man was in the state of fright and he faltered again. *'Don't stay in mute'* yelled Vedha. *'Sir... They are not good. They misused our girls. They took the girls and tried to involve them in prostitution. Rudra saved the girls and got them back.* ' said the man. *'Who is this Rudra?'* questioned Vedha. ' *The man who was hitting the secretaries in the footage.'* replied the man. ' *Why didn't you inform this to police?'* asked V edha. *'Rudra advised us not to complain.'* said the man.

Vedha stared at him anxiously, *'Where is Rudra now?'* asked Vedha. *'He has now left to his native'* replied the man. Vedha remained silent and thought deeply. ' *Sir, Rudra is a gentle man. He has a good helping nature. He is the saviour for all of us.'* said a granny who came to clean the room. V edha smiled at her, *'Okay sir! Thank you for your co-operation.'* he said to the man and left from the office. Anamika followed him and got into the car. Anamika was looking moody, *'What happened to you?'* he asked. *'No Bhaiya! I was thinking about this case. We have no leads'* she replied. *'Yes Ana! Stay calm. The suspect cannot hold on for more days. He'll definitely miss something. We are close to that. Be patient!'* he said. Anamika was mazed about the crime and her mind was flooded with Rudra's thoughts. *'Ana! I'll drop you in home. I've got a meeting with my higher officials.'* said Vedha. *'Okay Bhaiya!'* she said. Vedha drove to home and left Anamika. Anamika entered the house, Mom ran to her, *'Ana! How was your day?'* she asked in delight. *'It was awesome ma. I had good time with Bhaiya'* she said with a smile. Mom smiled in return, *'Come! Have your lunch'* she said and served the food. *'I feel tired. I will sleep for a while'* she said and went to her room. Her mind was flooded with random thoughts, after few minutes she fell asleep.

It was 5 pm , Vedha returned back to home. *'Why are you so late Vedha?'* asked Mom. *'I had an important meeting today ma'* he said. *'Did you have your lunch?'* she asked. *'Not yet. Feeling really hungry'* he said in exhaustion. *'Okay go and get refreshed.'* she said. Vedha washed his face and palms. He got seated, then M om served him. *'Where is the criminologist?'* he asked. *'She is sleeping from afternoon. She said that she is feeling tired '* she said. ' *She is not tired. She is thinking deeply about the case'* he r eplied. *'She is a young girl, that's why'* replied Mom. ' *Yeah. I'm sure she is having a great future.'* he said proudly. *'Definitely! She is ambitious.'* replied Mom happily.

Few hours passed, Anamika walked out from the room, *'Here comes the sleeping beauty'* yelled Vedha. Anamika chuckled. *'How was your meeting?'* asked Anamika. *'See her, still thinking about the case.'* said Vedha. Anamika smiled. *'We got a blur image of a suspect . He was seen in a clash with the footballer in the parking area of the roadhouse.'* said Vedha. *'Good. This is our first lead. Can you show me his image.'* she asked. 'Sure. *Go and g e t my file from the car'* he said. Anamika ran and brought the file to him. Rudra took the image and gave it to her .

Anamika gave a startled look and got paused after seeing the image , *'Ana!, Why are you peering? Your eyes are turning into a microscope.'* he replied with a laugh. *' No Bhaiya'* she stammered. Vedha grabbed the image and said, *'Enough! Go and relax yourself'.*

Anamika went back to her room. *' Her behaviour is really freaky '* s aid Shamala . *'I'll see to it'* replied Vedha. After few minutes, Vedha headed to Anamika's room, he found her standing in the balcony. *'Oii'* yelled Vedha. Anamika jerked. *' Ana! You're making a mountain out of a mole hill. Just overthinking of something. '* asked Vedha. She remained silent. *'You can share me if something troubled your mind.'* he said with a pat in her head. Anamika burst into tears, *'Bhaiya!'* she cried. *'What happened dear?'* she asked. *'Listen to me, I was in love with Rudra, the guy who was in clash with the secretaries.'* she cried. *' What?'* replied Vedha in shock. *'And one more thing, the image which you showed, looks alike Rudra'* she sobbed. *'This is really staggering '* he replied. *'I'm really perplexed'* she cried. *'Ana! S ay everything, right from the starting.'* he said. Anamika explained the whole story. *'Oh my god'* he replied with a sigh.

Anamika's chin dropped down. *'I've no words to say. Let's probe into his environment and check if something connects..... And I don't think he will be the killer as he is having a good picture.'* he replied.

Anamika agreed. *'Don't think about this too much. Be relaxed!'* he advised and left from her room. Anamika was sleepless that night, she was thinking about Rudra's suspicion.

6.2 Leads to Leads

Next day, Caesar was lying queasy. *'He is sick, I think we should take him to the veterinarian'* said Anamika. *'Okay! Get him into the car, let's visit the veterinary clinic before leaving to work.'* said Vedha. Anamika and Vedha left to the clinic, and Caesar was treated. *'Now, we'll leave to your boyfriend's villa.'* said Vedha. Anamika nodded her head. The car headed to the villa, Vedha and Anamika got down the call. *'Let's call the owner of this villa '* said Vedha. *'I've done this once, so better you make a call. If I do, he may lead to doubt.'* replied Anamika. *'Yes'* replied Vedha and dialled to the owner. *'I'm Rudra's friend. I visited him, but he is not available.'* said Vedha. *' Yes, h e vacated the house.'* said the owner. *'Do you know his current address?'* he asked. *'Actually, I'm living in Canada. I got connected with Rudra through OLX, my brother was maintaining my properties and he arranged this villa for Rudra. Rudra just lived there for a month, now he said that he is leaving to his native. This is why, I think several times to give my house to a bachelor s ,.... Later h e asked for a help, he asked us to shift the packaged things in the house to Hyderabad.... My brother is helping natured, he shifted his things as per his instruction... I've that address only. His phone number is also unavailable. Please don't disturb me by enquiring about th at man, I've received several calls. Inform this to your friends. '* narrated the owner. *' Sorry for the trouble. His father and brother was ill, so he took them to his native.'* bluffed Rudra. *'What? Rudra was living alone in my villa.'* replied the owner. *'Yes sir!.... His father and brother was living with his sister, now he took all of them to his native.'* bluffed Rudra with a stammer. *'Alright! I will text you the address where we sent the things '* said the man. *'Thank you'* replied Vedha and ended the call. *'This man is a blatherskite. Anyway he helped us'* said Vedha with a chuckle. Anamika giggled. Vedha's phone popped a notification, he peeked, *'Here comes the address'* said Vedha. Vedha giggled, *'Your boyfriend has moved to other state'* he said. *'Where?'* asked Anamika. *'Hyderabad, Telangana'* replied Vedha.

' Come, lets go inside.' he said with a wink. *'It's locked, how can we get in?'* she asked. *'Just follow me. I'll open the door'* h e replied. T hey entered in to the villa, Caesar was barking furiously, *'Stay calm Caesar! Don't get us into trouble.'* he yelled. They walked in, *'Give your bobby pins'* he asked with a giggle. Anamika gave a shocked look, then she removed the pins from h er hair and gave him. Vedha stretched the pin straight, then he inserted one of the pin into the lock's hole, with other pin he was poking the lock. After few pokes,   the lock released.   Then he took his wallet and took a magnetic card. *' What is this?'* she asked. *'Ushhh... It is an expired card from food court'* he whispered. 'Brainy!' she chuckled. Then, h e inserted the magnetic card in the gap of the door's opening and pushed   out   the metal lock. The door opened,   *'Hurrah!'* he e xclaimed. Anamika chuckled,   *'You   have   opened the door like a professional burglar.'* she   said. They entered in and hunted, but the place looked spick and span. Caesar jumped out from the car's window, h e ran to the backyard and was barking furiously. *' Caesar is messing up'* s aid Anamika. 'Caesar! Caesar!' yelled Vedha and followed the rugged German Shepherd. Caesar l ooked eerie, he was rushing in front of a small room. *'We should open this room'* said Vedha. He gave a hard push, but it didn't open. *'The door is ceased'* he said and ran to his car. He brought a screw-driver and pierced in the door's gap.   The door opened after a stiff push. The duo entered the room. It looked clean and tidy. But, Anamika sneezed. *' It smells unusual'* he said. *'Yeah! Kinda chemical's smell'* said Anamika and made a series of storm-like sneezes. Vedha thought d eeply. Then he called to one of his friend, *'Vedha here!... Jenny, Are you free today?'* he asked. *'Yes, I'm on off today.'* replied

Jenny. *'Can you come to a spot, I'm on an investigation of a very important case. We need your help.'* he asked. *'Sure Vedha, Text me the address, I'll follow.'* she replied. After few moments, Jenny reached them. *'She is Jenny, a brilliant forensic analyst. She'll inspect this place thoroughly.'* he said. Anamika smiled at her. Jenny took her examination kit, she left into the villa and started her investigation.

A namika and Vedha walked around the backyard, *'Have you been here before?'* he ask ed. *'No Bhaiya! I've been only till the front space.'* she replied. They noticed Caesar' s fury did not settle, he was scrambling on the ground. *'Caesar sensed something'* he said. After an hour of scrutiny, Jenny arrived, *'I will give you the results in two hours. I've found some fingerprints in the villa and the backyard room is subjected to some chemicals. I will give you a clean report and analysis of the used chemicals. I will also produce the patterns of the fingerprint s found '* she said. *'Thank you Jenny!'* he said.

The trio explored, Caesar was uncontrollable, Jenny went near him. *'Vedha!'* she yelled. Anamika and Vedha ran to her, *'Yeah!'* he replied. *'See this particular piece of land, it is uneven. Someone had dug and covered it again.'* she said. *'I will spade here.'* he said. Anamika gave the spade which was lying on the ground. After continuous digs, they found something like a bundle. The bundle caused an unbearable stinky smell. Anamika and Jenny covered their nose, *'Move away'* yelled V edha. He took the bundle from the pit and threw it above the land. He tore the covering of the bundle with his pocket knife. *' It is a dead d og!'* he yelled with a long breathe.

They were shocked, the dog was beaten brutally and i t's paw was chopped. Anamika screamed, *'It is Rudra's Dog'* she cried. V edha was astounded. *'What?'* he asked in shock. *'Yes. I've seen this dog here. He was having two adult Rottweilers. This is one of that.'* she cried. *'Calm down '* he said and Jenny warmed her. *' You both stay here. I'll dispose this bundle and come back .'* he said. Then he took the bundle and left from there. *'Are you scared?'* asked Jenny. *'Yes, terribly.'* replied Anamika .

After few minutes, Vedha returned back to the spot, *'Lets get out from here fast.'* he said and levelled the land back. He closed the doors and fixed back the lock in the front door. The trio and the dog left from there after retrieving the traces. V edha looked tensed and Anamika remained silent. *'Lets go to my lab. I'll test these samples and give you the results.'* said Jenny. *'Yes, I'm heading there.'* he said. The y reached to her lab, Jenny started her testing, Anamika and Vedha was waiting out, *'Bhaiya! Why are you tensed?'* she aske d. *'I'm thinking '* he replied. *' Rudra has a good heart, but something is mysterious.'* she said. *'How can he have a good heart? He disguised and cheated you.'* he replied anxiously. Anamika remained silent. *'He is a bloody cold blooded murderer.'* he yelled anxiously. *'Sorry Bhaiya!'* she replied said in a low tone. *'Why should you feel sorry?'* he asked. Jenny came, *' In the backyard, t he floor is washed with Hydrogen Peroxide and Ammonia, these are usually used to remove blood stains. And the walls are white- washed, the knobs, windows, walls are sprayed and wiped with iodine, ninhydrin, cyanoacrylate solutions which is used to get rid of fingerprints. Then, I've also produced a fingerprint pattern which was found abundantly '* she said and gave him the test results. *' Thank you Jenny!'* replied Vedha. *' He is a genius. Why should an ordinary man do such stuffs while vacating his house?'* asked Jenny. *'Yes! You're absolutely right '* he replied. Jenny nodded her head. *' I want to handle this case in clandestine. So, this is gonna be an undercover project. Rudra should not guess that we are reaching him.'* said V edha. Jenny and Anamika agreed.

Vedha and Anamika returned to home. Anamika's life had a thunderstorm shock, she was unable to digest the truth. According to her, Rudra was a good-hearted charming man. She was unable to accept that he was a brutal murderer.

Chapter-7

7.1 Childhood in Agony

Next day, ' We' ve to know more about him to puzzle out his intension behind his attacks.' *said Vedha.* 'Yes, What should we do now?' *asked Anamika.* 'We will go and enquire Rudra's past from the care-taker in Swarga charity.' *h e said.*

Both left to the charity, 'How can I help you, sir? *asked the old man.* 'We want to know more about Rudra ' *said Vedha.* 'What did he do? ' *asked the man.* 'We got to know about the dead secretaries only, we need to know about Rudra too' *said Vedha.* 'How is Rudra connected in this case?' *asked the man in shock.* 'Stop questioning me, just answer my questions.' *bawled Vedha.* 'Okay sir' *r eplied the man in fright.* 'Go ahead' *said Vedha.* ' Rudra came here at his age of seventeen. He was transferred from a charity in Chennai. H e was good in studies. He does not like to work under any firms, he was having dreams of starting his own business. He is good-hearted, he is an incarnation of Karna. He is very generous. He was earning through share market. ' *said the man.* ' Where he living? Was he living with anybody?' *asked Vedha.* 'No. We got to know he is living in Kalina.... He lives alone.' *replied the man.* 'Okay. Give me the details of his previous charity.' *asked Vedha.* ' Okay sir' *replied the man, he wrote the address in a piece of paper and gave it to Vedha.* 'Thank you! We're leaving' *said Vedha. Anamika and Vedha got back to the car and left from there.*

' What is our next move?' *asked Anamika.* 'We are leaving to Chennai and reaching to his previous charity. We should know his past.' *said Vedha.* 'Great' *replied Anamika.*

Next day, Anamika and Vedha left to Chennai. They lodged in an inn. That evening, they left to the charity and met the care-taker. 'I'm the deputy superintendent of Mumbai. I want to enquire about Rudra, who was shifted from here to Swarga Charity.' *said Vedha.* 'Sure sir' *said the lady and checked her system.* 'Can you say me the year when he was transferred ?' *asked the lady.* '2005' *he replied. The lady bobbed,* 'Rudra got a scholarship to study in a university in Mumbai. So, he was transferred there.' *she said.* ' Okay Ma'am. How was his childhood? How did he come here?' *he asked.* 'Hmm... I'm employed here from 2010, I have no idea about him.' *replied the lady.* 'Can you give me the contact of the previous care-taker?' *he asked.* 'Sure' *she replied and shared the address.*

Anamika noticed a photograph hanging on the wall, it was a photograph of old man and a small boy. Below the photograph, it was written George and Alan. Anamika was shocked, ' Bhaiya!' *she called and showed that photograph to Vedha.* 'Who is that in the photograph?' *he asked in shock.* 'Father George, our founder. Alan, his son.' *replied the lady.* 'How did they pass away?' *asked Vedha.* 'Alan is a special kid. Father loves him. Before few years, Alan passed away due to his health issues. Father was despondent after his death. The toll o n his heart took away his life, he died in sleep. It was a heart arrest.' *she replied in agony.* 'I'm sorry' *replied Vedha. The lady smiled.* 'Thank you Ma'am. We're leaving.' *he said and they left from there.*

' Now again, we should follow an other person to know everything. ' *said Anamika tiredly.* ' W e' re now like scavengers' *he replied.* 'We' ll have our dinner and leave to the inn. We'll resume this tomorrow.' *he said.* ' Okay ' *she replied.* 'Are you hungry?' *asked Vedha.* 'Obviously' *she replied. They moved forward and stopped to a Rickshaw driver,* 'Can you say us a good restaurant in this city ?' *he asked. The man stared, he did not understand the language. Anamika laughed, 'Just google it Bhaiya!' she said. Vedha searched for the best hotel in Chennai, he got " Adayar Anandha Bavan" in result. They reached to the restaurant and the waiter listed the food items. The food items were totally new to them,* 'What is the best food of this restaurant ?' *he asked.* 'Poori & masal, Pongal, Vada, Masal Dosa' *listed the waiter.* 'G ive us one from all the dishes' *replied Vedha.*

After few minutes, 'You know something, one day, Me and Rudra had dinner together. That day, we ordered many dishes like today.... It was during Dada's admission in hospital... Actually, Rudra was the one who helped us at the right time. His picture was like a gem. I did not dream about this.' *expressed Anamika.* 'Love is blind. It is not your fault' *he replied. Anamika smiled.* 'It makes you blind. I f your heart fell for a person, their flaws will be invisible. Even now, if you have love d him truly, your heart tends to favour him.' *said Vedha.* 'More than favouring, I'm unable to accept this' *she replied.* 'I understand' *he replied. The food arrived to their table. They had great time in tasting the new cuisine.*

The day ended. It was a hectic travel in a new city for them. travelling to know the past.

Next day, they visited the ex-caretaker's house. A lady opened the door and enquired them. 'Yes, sir. My father was the caretaker of that charity. But now, he is not well. He is suffering from Alzheimer's disease. I'm not sure, how far he'll co-operate with you.' *she said.* 'I understand. Let' s try' *replied Vedha.* 'Sure sir. Please come in.' *she welcomed and took them inside. The lady lifted the old man and made him to sit,* 'Appa! Someone has come to see you' *she said. The old man greeted them with a smile.* 'Do you know Rudra?' *she asked. The man remained silent and thought for a while,* 'Yes, of course' *replied the man.* 'When did you see him last?' *he asked.* 'Long Back! I sent him far away' *said the man nervously.* 'Cool sir...' *he said. The lady gave a glass of water to the man.* 'Why did you send him away?' *he asked. The man's face turned red,* 'He is the best! Best of all!..... He punished the molester, Raj. Raj.... sexually assaulted the girls of our charity. Rudra pushed him from the terrace... I saw that. Raj died on head injury... I made actions to shift Rudra from our charity to save his future. Finally, I applied for a scholarship. He wa s selected to study in Mumbai.' *cried the man. The lady calmed and consoled the man.*

'How did Rudra c ome to your charity?' *he asked.* 'One day, Father George saw him fainted in the road. Rudra was starved and weak. Father found that Rudra was isolated from his family so he was brought to the charity.' *replied the man.* 'Do you know anyone from his family?' *asked Vedha. The man thought for minutes,* 'Once, a girl reached him. She was his sister. But I don't remember her name.' *replied the man.* 'Can I get her contact details?' *he asked. The man was thinking, he was unable to respond.* 'Sir, we can search in his old registers.' *said the lady.* 'Thank You' *replied Vedha. The lady brought the old registers, Anamika helped her in searching. After turning the pages for an hour, they found the entry. The girl's name was Devi. Anamika noted her phone number. Vedha and Anamika thanked and left from there.*

'Bhaiya! There is a connection i n Rudra's murders. He is attacking men who assault women sexually. His first attack was on Raj, a molester . The n the secretaries were also blamed on the same fact .' *she said.* 'You're right Ana! This may be the reason behind his attacks.' *he replied.* 'Now, lets try to call that girl.' *said Vedha. Anamika giggled,* ' Now she'll not be a girl, she'll will be a lady' *she said.* 'Too much of brain' *he exclaimed. They called Devi,* 'Hello, I'm Vedha, superintendent of police. Am I speaking to Devi?' *asked Vedha.* 'Yes, sir. I'm Devi.' *she replied.* 'We need to enquire about a person to you, it is official. How can we reach you?' *he asked.* 'You can say me your destination sir, I'll be there' *she replied. Vedha shared the address of the inn to her.*

After an hour, Devi arrived there. 'Hello sir, I'm Devi' *she introduced.* 'Please be seated' *said Vedha.* 'How can I help you sir?' *she asked.*

'Do you know Rudra?' *he asked. The lady became emotional,* 'Yes, He is my brother' *she replied.* 'We know. Where is he now?' *he asked.* 'I don't know. We lost him at his age of five.' *she replied.* 'How was he lost?' *he asked.* 'He ran from our mother's funeral' *she cried.* 'I'm sorry.... Please, c an you explain us his childhood in detail?' *he asked.* 'It is a melancholy. Our mother wa s an innocent lady. My father was a wealthy man. My Mom was abused by father always. He used to hit her brutally. He will lock me and Rudra in a room. O ur Mom's last days were real hell. S he was raped by many men who were sent by my father. My father used enjoy these scenes. He is a real monster. Rudra was depressed from very young age. Mom used to calm every time. One day, Mom was unable to bear her pain. S he h ung herself when we were sleeping. We w ere shocked to see her hanging in the ceiling. Rudra sobbed after seeing Mom in the freezer box. He ran from the funeral, we did not notice. We filed a complaint on his missing. We tried hard to find him. But we couldn't...' *she cried. Anamika cried silently after hearing from her.* ' I'm sorry Ma'am. I made you emotional.' *consoled Vedha.* ' Don't worry about it ' *she said and wiped her tears.* 'One request. If you find him, say that I'm yearning to see him once. I pray for him everyday.' *she said with a painful smile. Anamika took her phone and showed his photograph,* ' Aww... He is a grown-up now ' *she exclaimed. Anamika smiled.* 'Can you share me this picture?' *she aske d.* 'Sure' *replied Anamika. Later, Devi left from there.*

Anamika and Vedha left back to their city carrying all the truth.

7.2 Series of kills

That day, Vedha was in a meeting with his higher officials. The commissioner hosted the session, 'The city is facing a funk. Do you all remember the murder of the secretaries in Swarga charity?' *he asked.* 'Yes' *replied the officials.* 'The murder of the secretaries is similar to another murder. Murder of a footballer has the similar patterns of attack. ' *he said and display ed the presentation. The officials listened to him carefully. Vedha nodded,* "Anamika found this long back" *he thought.* 'Not only two such murders, there are nearly 13 murders in similar patterns found so far. ' *said the commissioner. Vedha was shocked,* "It was only six to my knowledge, but he is saying thirteen. 2 secretaries, the footballer and three men...... Oh my god! " *he thought. The commissioner displayed images of the murders in the slide.* 'The suspect is hammering the victims to knock them down. Then the victim is subjected to series of stabs all around the body. The main strike of h is attack is amputating the arm of the victims. Every victim's arm is missing. M ain point is, if the victim is right-handed, the suspect is amputating the right arm and if the victim is left-handed, the suspect is amputating the left arm. T he suspect is targeting only men. So far, we did not find any woman attacked in this pattern. ' *explained the commissioner. V edha was shocked to know the new facts about Rudra,* "He is dangerous" *he thought.* 'We have a single clue, the footballer was engaged in a clash in the tavern. A man brutally attacked him a fter the footballer miss behaved with a lady in the club. We have a blur image of that man. The man may or may not be the suspect.' *said the commissioner.* 'It is just a prediction' *said an officer.* 'Yes. We're gonna release this image to the public and we should aware about this murders to the people.' *said the commissioner.* 'Sir! Releasing the image will cause tension among the people. We have no strong leads on the suspect. What if the man in the image is not the suspect?' *asked one of the officer.* 'Thanks for the advise. But we should aware the people. A blur image will not affect a person's life. If the person in the image is not the suspect, he'll surrender to u s and the original suspect will a ttack lethargically. If the person in the image is the suspect, he'll be stunned. His attacks will be collapsed. Even people will report to us if he is known to them. Somehow, the release of image can help us. ' *replied the commissioner.*

The session ended and the image was produced to the press. The city witnessed a great focus and tension on this case. V edha left back to his home. Anamika ran to him, 'Bhaiya! What is this? The image Rudra is spreading as a wild fire.' *she replied in shock.* 'Yes, I know. But this is the decision of the higher officials.' *he replied. Anamika's face shrunk.* 'Did you reveal about Rudra?' *she asked.* 'No' *he replied.* 'Why?' *she asked.* 'His story was heart wrenching. I was unable to reveal it. I've never felt like this before in my service.' *he said.* 'Yes!' *replied Anamika.* 'He is dangerous too. There are totally 13 murders found in the same pattern' *he said. Anamika was shocked,* 'What?' *she asked.* 'Yes! I will show you the files' *he said and explained her.* 'Bhaiya! This is scaring.' *she replied after seeing the presentation.* What should we do now?' *asked Anamika.* 'W e should w ait' *he replied.* 'What?' *she asked.* 'We should wait for his next move. According to our assumption, he is somewhere near Hyderabad. We should keep an eye on cases occurred there' *he said.* 'Okay Bhaiya! ' *she replie d*

' You both will not stop discussing about your official topics. Won't you get bored?' *asked Shamala.* 'Ma! Anamika is worried about h er boyfriend.' *said Vedha with a laugh. Anamika spooked, the she signed him to stop.* 'Ana! Is that true? Who is that? ' *asked Shamala.* 'Vedha is blabbering' *stammered Anamika.* 'Ye s M a ! I was kidding her.' *he said. Mom smiled and left to the kitchen.* 'Why are you scaring me?' *whispered Anamika. Vedha chuckled,* 'Yeah! You r boyfriend is the city's trending murder.' *he replied. Anamika's chin dropped down,* 'I'm not in love any more' *she replied sadly.* 'This is unfair.' *he replied with a huge laugh. That day ended. One month passed, There were no such murders. V edha was totally confused about his instincts. He took leave on his duty.* 'I'm leaving to Hyderabad.' *he said to Anamika.* 'For what?' *she asked.* 'I'm reaching to the address given by the villa owner ' *said Vedha.* 'Alright! Why are you b othered now? You' ve other important cases, right! And n ow, there are no such murders occurring.' *asked Anamika.* ' I know, I've many other cases, still this case is really dangerous.' *he replied.* ' Bhaiya! Yo u're over-thinking' *she replied.* ' Ana! This case is affecting my peace ' *he replied and sighed.* 'I'm also coming with you.' *she replied.* 'Not this time' *he said.* 'No way. I'll be with you every time' *she replied with a pinch. Vedha shut his eyes and mouth, and took a long breathe.* 'Everything is irritating' *he said and sighed.* 'I think, you' re also in love with Rudra. Thinking of him all time.' *she said with a huge laugh. V edha left to his room and locked the door loudly.* 'What happened to him?' *asked Mom. Anamika giggled,* 'Bhaiya has gone made' *she replied.* 'Crazy girl!' *s aid Mom. The day ended*

Two days later, Anamika and Vedha went to Hyderabad. They reached to the address and found a bungalow. Then they knocked, a man opened the door. cv 'I'm Vedha, superintendent of Police, Mumbai city. Do you know Rudra?' *asked Vedha.* 'Hello sir... Yes, I know him. He is my pal.' *replied the man.* 'Alright! We traced a parcel delivery address of him. That's how we reached you.' *said Vedha.* 'Yes sir. Rudra wa s stuck in his native. He vacated his house from Mumbai and was shifting to Hyderabad. H e asked me for a help, he said me to collect the packaged things from packers and movers. And I did it.' *informed the man.* ' Okay!.... Then how did you return the things back?' *asked Vedha.* 'He came in a wagon and collected the things from me.' *replied the man.* 'Do you know his current address?' *asked Vedha.* 'No sir. He was in urge so he left fast. He said that he'll reach to me later after getting settled.' *informed the man.* 'Thank you for the co-operation sir' *said Vedha.*

Later, Anamika and Vedha checked in a hotel and they settled in their suite. 'It feels like a perfect vacation' *said Anamika. Vedha stared,* 'We're not here to enjoy and you know that.' *he said.* 'I know this but I don't know the purpose of being here. I've no idea about how w e' re going to proceed further?' *said Anamika.* 'I always trust my intuition. Definitely we're leading closer. Stay calm! We'll surely find a solution. ' *he replied.*

Chapter-8

8.1 The New Normal

Next day, ' Good morning, Bhaiya!' *called Anamika with a smile and a cup of coffee.* ' You've w oke up so early?' *asked Vedha, rubbing his eyes.* 'Yes, I'm super-excited' *replied Anamika. Anamika walked to him and gave a cup of coffee.* 'Boss............. Birla Mandir, Hussain sagar, Chowmahalla palace, Charminar, Golconda fort etc., a re the places to be visited in this city' *she said with a wide smile. Vedha was annoyed ,* 'We're not going anywhere' *he replied.* 'Then, how're we going to find the murderer?' *she asked. Vedha ignored her words and looked into his mobile.* 'Bhaiya!' *she yelled loudly . But, Vedha remained still,* 'Don't do this.. Take me out. How will you find Rudra by staying here?' *whined Anamika.* ' To find Rudra, we have to roam around the town and not in the tourist spots' *he replied and smiled wide.* 'Don't smile' *said Anamika and sat o n the couch angrily.*

After few moments, Vedha took bath and called Anamika. 'You go and roam, I'm not gonna come' *yelled Anamika.* 'Aren't you excited meet your boyfriend after long time?' *asked Vedha with a laugh.* 'Not at all! And you know something, nowadays you are yearning to meet him' *said Anamika.* 'Definitely' *he said.* 'Okay Ana! You stay here, I will go. I promise you to take you out at the evening' *he said with a pat in her head. Anamika smiled. Rudra left from the hotel and headed to the commissioner's office.* 'I'm from Mumbai, superintendent of police. I want an appointment to meet the assistant commissioner' *said Vedha to the constable.* 'Sure sir. He will be available here at 11pm today.' *replied the constable. Vedha sat on the bench and took the lying newspaper near him.* ' Sir, do you prefer to have tea to coffee?' *asked the constable.* 'Tea' *he replied with a smile.*

Vedha was noticing the environment of the station. The station was busy, people were coming in and out. It was around 11 pm , the assistant commissioner reached there. The constable went to the his cabin and informed about Vedha's arrival. The assistant commissioner came out of his cabin, 'Dude!' *he called Vedha and gave hug.* 'How are you man?' *asked Vedha.* 'I'm good. What about you?' *replied the officer.* ' I'm good man' *replied.* 'What made you to visit here?' *asked the officer.* 'It's really confidential and very important' *said Vedha.* 'Alright. I'll be free after one hour. We'll discuss then ' *he said.* 'Great man. I'll wait for you.' *said Vedha.*

After an hour, the officer came, 'Yeah dude. Come lets go out. It has been five years since meeting you.' *he said. Both left to the inn , Vedha knocked the door. Anamika opened the door,* 'Bhaiya! You c ame soon' *she said in shock. Vedha smiled,* ' He is Viswa, my friend. He is the assistant commissioner of Hyderabad' *he said.* 'Hello sir, I'm Anamika.' *she introduced and welcomed them. They entered in the suite and started their discussion.* ' Do you know about a serial killer who was trending last month?' *asked Vedha.* 'Yes. I remember. T hey also released an image of him' *sai d Viswa, the officer.* ' You're r ight!' *replied Vedha.* 'It was the hot topic of the country last month.' *said Viswa.* 'Yes, people forget the old topic when the new fire comes.' *said Vedha.* 'True' *replied Viswa.* ' You know something, we know the person behind those murders. To our guess, he is currently in Hyderabad' *said Vedha. Viswa got shocked.* 'We want to know the deaths occurred in Hyderabad, which is similar to the pattern of his attack.' *said Vedha.* 'I'm sure, there are no similar attack in this city.' *replied Viswa.* 'Okay. I'll explain the leads of this case, keep an eye on this. If something connect s , let me know.' *informed Vedha. Then he showed the case files of Rudra and explained their investigation and guesses to Viswa.* ' Oh! I understood it's seriousness. I'll surely concentrate on this' *replied Viswa. Vedha thanked him.* 'And, for how many days you guys going to be here?' *asked Viswa.* ' Probably, this week we're leaving . Looking for some leads.' *replied Vedha.* 'You can contact me anytime if you need any help' *said Viswa.* 'Who is this girl?' *he asked, pointing on Anamika. Vedha narrated the ir beautiful tale of bond.* 'Woah! This is phenomenal. You both are really lucky.' *said Viswa.* 'Thank you brother' *e xclaimed Anamika. Later, Viswa left the hotel.*

After two days, Vedha got a call, 'Hey dude. I'm Viswa. I got to know about a murder which occurred yesterday in Vizianagaram, Andhra Pradesh.' *he said.* 'Hi Viswa.... Okay, Then?' *e nquired Vedha.* 'A wealthy merchant and his sister-in-law was burnt alive. According to the autopsy report, the man has various stab all over his body. To my shock , his left arm is missing.' *said Viswa.* 'Oh my god! This is really terrific.' *shocked Vedha.* 'Yes dude. I feel, in some way this murder connects Rudra's style of attack.' *said Viswa.* ' Yeah! Let's go to Vizianagaram and check further .' *replied Vedha.* 'I'm coming to your inn in some time. L et's leave together to the spot' *said V iswa .* 'Okay dude... sure! ' *replied Vedha.*

After some time, Viswa reached and the trio left to the spot. 'I've informed to the department about our arrival. They accepted and they've arranged for an enquiry with the victim's wife.' *said Viswa.* 'G ood job dude' *said Vedha. Viswa smiled.* 'The criminologist is always in deep thinking. Silent all the time.' *said Viswa looking at Anamika. Vedha giggled,* 'This is first time for Anamika, a person calling her silent.' *he said. Anamika stared at Vedha,* 'No brother. I was a non-stop talker. Life is not a bed of roses, I had many losses, many disheartening and many disappointments. Nowadays, I became silent.' *replied Anamika.* 'I'm sorry. I made you emotional.' *consoled Viswa.* ' No! ' *she replied with a smile. Vedha looked at her and smiled back.*

They reached to the investigation department, 'Good morning sir.' *wished the inspector.* 'Good morning. He is Vedha, deputy superintendent of police. We need an enquiry with the victim's wife.' *said Viswa.* 'Hello sir. I got the instruction. Please follow me, I will take you to the investigation cabin.' *said the inspector and took them to cabin. Vedha and Viswa sat opposite to the victim's wife. Anamika stood in the glass chamber along with the inspector and watched their conversation.* 'Hello ma'am, I'm really sorry for your loss. But, we have to speak about this. We should find the murderer. I want your co-operation.' *said Vedha.* 'Sure sir' *replied the lady.* 'Don't hide anything from us. Say everything right from the beginning' *said Viswa. The lady nodded.* 'Go ahead' *said Vedha.*

The lady drank from the glass of water. 'Sir, my name is Devika. My husband is a famous business man in the city. Last week, I was not in the city. I was in my native. I got a news that my Husband and sister was burnt alive in our garage.' *said the lady.* 'Do you've doubt on anyone?' *asked Vedha.* 'No sir. I have no clue' *replied the lady.* 'Can you get me the video footage of the garage?' *asked Vedha.* 'I've already produced it to the department' *replied the lady.* 'Viswa, lets play it now.' *said Vedha.* 'Okay Vedha' *said Viswa and called the constable. The constable arranged the projector for playing the footages.* 'Let's start playing the footages from the day before the murder' *said Vedha. The footage was played, the garage was situated behind their bungalow. The back space of the house considered the parking space and a stock room. There was a steel staircase taking to a small single room and it was locked. The footage was normal, the work was going smooth. There was no chaos.* 'That's all for that day.' *said Viswa.* 'Let's play the footage on the day of murder.' *said Vedha. Footage was played, the day continued without any confusions. But the footage was corrupted and dead at 7:17 PM.* 'What happened?' *asked Vedha.* 'The camera in the garage was malfunctioning, this happens often. I was saying my husband to replace it. But h e ignored as he was always busy.' *informed the lady.* 'Okay ma'am' *replied Vedha.* 'That's all for that day? Do we have any footages left?'

asked Vedha. 'Yes Vedha. The next camera footages are starting from next day, 4 AM.' *said Viswa.* 'Okay' *said Vedha and played the footages. The next footages were also smooth, no doubtable scenes. Vedha stopped the video,* 'Who is staying in this room?' *asked Vedha pointing the single room.* 'One of our driver stays there, he was homeless so we arranged that room for him.' *informed the lady.* 'Viswa, take a shot of this scene in the footage' *said Vedha.* 'Sure Vedha' *replied Viswa and saved the shot.* 'Share the details of that driver. Where is he staying now?' *asked Vedha.* 'He is not here, he took leave from the work last week.' *replied the lady.* 'Do you have any governmental proofs of him?' *asked Vedha.* 'No sir, he said his documents are in his native. He assured us to produce it after a month.' *said the lady.* ' You're running a firm, t hese are really important. You should've the identity proofs of your workers' *said Vedha.* 'We ' ll maintain this strictly sir, we never fail to collect the proofs from our workers. But, this man, he was suffering. He was homeless and jobless. I suggested him to my husband.' *said the lady.* 'Oh... Where did you meet him first?' *asked Vedha.* 'I was taking my daughter to hospital, she was sick that day. Our car got repaired and stopped. He came and helped us. I saw him, his knee was bleeding. I asked him to join as we were going to hospital. He agreed and h e got his first-aid. I consulted the doctor for my daughter. Later, I enquired about him. He said that he was new to the city and he was homeless and jobless. So, I said him to come next day and gave my address. I suggested him to my husband and we offered him a job as a driver.' *said the lady.* 'How long he is working under your firm?' *asked Vedha.* 'Around twenty days' *replied the lady.*

Vedha became and thought deeply, then, 'Viswa, come out' *he called. Viswa followed him.* 'Ma'am, wait here for some moments. We'll be back' *said Vedha. The lady nodded. Vedha took Viswa out,* 'Dude, take a peer on the shot where I said you to pause. O n previous day of the m urder,   t he single room' s lock was locked. And the lock was open fro m 3 PM on the day of murder. Again, it was locked at 4 AM on the next day' *said Vedha.* 'I understand' *replied Viswa.* 'Are you getting, what I meant to say? ' *asked Vedha.* 'Yes dude' *replied Viswa.* 'You'll be clear if you notice virtually. Come, let's have replay' *said Vedha. Vedha and Viswa left to the class chamber, and played the sequences in the computer. They noticed a man entering the room around 2:45 PM. He carried a baggage from the room and left from the garage. The man left the door unlocked. The man was dressed in jacket covering his head so they were unable capture his face. Vedha and Viswa went back to the lady.* 'Can you identify this person?' *asked Vedha and showed the shot of the man in the footage. The lady peered,* 'I think it was our driver. Because, no one had the key of the room and no one will have the necessity to go that room.' *replied the lady.* 'Are you sure?' *asked Vedha.* 'Yes, his physique also looks alike' *replied.* 'Do you know his name?' *asked Vedha.* 'Yes, his name is Shiva.' *replied the lady.*

' Ma'am, thank you for your co-operation. We're suspecting that your driver may be the murderer. W e want to investigate his room. So that we can figure out clearly.' *said Vedha.* 'I don't think so, he is new to us. But within this short period of time, he developed a good bond with us. My daughter is really fond on him. He is very affectionate. He calls me as sister. Once he said that I resemble his sister. He is a gem.' *said the lady.* ' Most of the murderers are ordinary people like us ' *replied Vedha.* ' Yes sir, I agree. You can make your investigation in that room' *said the lady.* 'Thank you!' *said Vedha. The meeting ended, the lady left. Anamika, Vedha and Viswa got in their car,* 'Bhaiya! How d id you say that the driver is the murderer?' *asked Anamika.* 'It is clear that he came to his room, cleared his evidences. Later he stopped the camera and executed his murder.' *replied Vedha.* ' He is tricky ' *exclaimed Anamika.* 'You have a sharp eyes dude' *said Viswa and tapped on his shoulders. Vedha smiled.*

They headed to the lady's house and walked to the single room in the garage. The trio hunted for the clues. The room consisted a bed and a study table. There were no belongings in the room. Anamika searched under the study table and she found a prescription. 'Bhaiya! I found this' *said Anamika and gave it to Vedha. Vedha looked deeply,* ' Oh! Th is person visits a psychiatrist.' *he said and kept the prescription in his pocket. They searched for further evidences. But nothing was suspicious rather than the prescription.* 'Viswa, order this place under prohibition. No one should enter this room.' *o rdered Vedha.* 'Okay dude' *said Vedha.* 'Now, we'll leave to this psychiatrist.' *replied Vedha.* 'Okay' *replied Viswa and Anamika.*

The trio headed to the psychiatrist's destination. The clinic was compact. It had beautiful paintings which calmed the mind. 'We want to meet the doctor.' *said Viswa to the receptionist.* ' Sure sir, I will register your appointment. Please fill this form.' *said the receptionist and gave the form to them.* 'Sir, we are not here for consulting him. We're from crime department. We want to enquire him.' *said Viswa.* 'Okay sir. I will inform him' *said the receptionist and dialled the psychiatrist.* 'Hello sir, We've got few cops to enquire you. They're asking for your appointment.' *said the receptionist over the call.* 'Okay daisy. I'll be there in 15 mins. Ask them to wait. Provide them beverages. I'm coming there soon.' *replied the doctor.* ' Sir, please be seated. Our doctor is arriving soon.' *said the lady. The trio sat in the hall and the lady provided them soft drinks.*

After few minutes the doctor arrived to the hospital, ' I'm Mr Devendra Reddy, chief psychiatrist. I was called for your appointment.' *said the psychiatrist.* 'Hello sir... We're from crime and investigation branch. We need some information of your patient.' *said Viswa.* 'Sure sir' *replied the doctor.* 'Daisy, come here' *called the doctor.* 'Yes sir' *replied the receptionist.* 'Ask them the details and find the patient in the system.' *ordered the doctor.* 'Okay sir. Please give us the details' *asked the receptionist.* 'We have a prescription... Here it is' *said Vedha and gave them the prescription.* 'Give me a minute' *replied the lady. He entered the patient ID and patient name in the system,* 'Sir, his name his Shiva.' *said the lady and took a print-out of his profile. She gave the profile to the doctor.* 'Please come to my cabin.' *called the doctor and took the trio to his room.* 'Please be seated' *said the doctor.*

The trio sat opposite to him. The doctor looked at the profile, 'Yes, I remember him. A young handsome man. He is suffering from Schizophrenia. He is undergoing symptoms of hallucinations, anxiety behaviour patterns and depression.' *informed the doctor.* 'Okay sir. How long he is taking his treatments' *asked Vedha.* 'He is suffering for five years. He was taking treatments in Maharastra. Now, he has moved to this city. So he is continuing the treatment with me.' *said the doctor.* 'Okay sir. Do you have any of his photograph? We want to see his face.' *said Vedha.* 'Hmm. I can get you the video footage recorded on his day of visit. ' *said the doctor.* 'Please...' *replied Vedha.*

The doctor bend down and took a hard-disk, he inserted the hard-disk in his system and searched for the footages. 'Here you go' *said the doctor and turned the monitor to them. The trio peered, they were shocked.* 'It is Rudra' *said Anamika.* 'Yes' *replied Vedha.* 'Thank you sir. I want a copy of these footages.' *asked Vedha.* ' Sure sir. You can take a copy of it' *replied the doctor.* 'And one more thing, if this person comes. Inform us. Don't say about our enquiry to him. This is confidential. He is an accused.' *said Vedha.* 'Definitely sir. I'll inform you . I'll follow your instructions.' *said the doctor.* 'Thank you!' *said Vedha and took the copy of the footage. Then the trio left the clinic.*

' He thinks himself as clever. He has left out his traces. We should find him soon.' *said Vedha.* ' I'm really scared of him. His brutality has increased. His last attack was really terrible.' *said Viswa.* 'Yes. He is very dangerous. We should find him soon.' *replied Vedha. Viswa left them in their inn and left back to his duty.*

8.2 Not So Cruel

Two days passed, Vedha and Anamika got a call that Mom was ill. She was admitted in hospital by their relative. *'Viswa, you take care of this case. I'm leaving to my city for an emergency. Beware of him and try to find him. I'll come later and continue my progress in this.'* said Vedha. *'Sure dude. Don't worry, I'll take care of this.'* replied Viswa. Later, Anamika and Vedha left to their city.

They went to the hospital and saw their Mom, *'Is your work completed?'* she asked. *'Yes ma. How are you now?'* asked Vedha. *'You both rushed here because of me'* replied Mom in a saddened tone. *'No ma. Don't think like this.'* said Vedha and held her hands. Mom smiled, *'Where is Ana?'* she asked. Anamika walked in, *'Hey Mom!'* she called with a smile. *'Ana!'* she exclaimed. *'You'll be fine. Don't worry.'* said Anamika and gave her a hug. Vedha and Anamika left out from Mom's ward. *'Bhaiya! Lets ask about Mom's condition to the doctor.'* said Anamika. *'Yes, that's right. Come on, lets go.'* he said and took her to the doctor's cabin. *'Excuse me sir.'* called Vedha. *'Please come in.'* replied the doctor. Anamika and Vedha sat before him. *'We want to know our Mom's condition.'* said Vedha. *'She is out of danger now. But you must be careful with her, she needs some special care. She should have her medicines regularly. Don't leave her alone in home, she is old now. Someone should be with her.'* said the doctor. *'Yes sir, we understand.'* replied Vedha. *'You can discharge her tomorrow.'* said the doctor. *'Thank you sir'* he said and they left his cabin. *'Bhaiya! Did you listen what he said? We should not leave Mom alone and we should take good care of her.'* said Anamika. *'Yes Ana! I understand. We should do something for sure. But how?'* he asked. *'We'll appoint a maid to take care of her.'* said Anamika. *'That's a good idea. I'll look for someone who m we can trust.'* replied Vedha. *'Okay Bhaiya! Let's find someone soon.'* said Anamika.

Next day, Mom was discharged from hospital and she was taken back to home. *'Bhaiya! I have my convocation next week. I received a mail today.'* said Anamika. *'Great. Officially, you are a master criminologist.'* replied Vedha. Anamika smiled. *'Hey listen. I found a perfect person to take care of our Mom.'* said Vedha. *'Who is that?'* asked Anamika. *'I've called her for an informal interview. I received her application yesterday.'* replied Vedha. *'Okay Bhaiya.'* replied

Anamika. *'She'll be arriving here in some time.'* informed Vedha. *'Cool!'* she replied and left to Mom's room. Anamika entered the room and sat on Mom's bed, *' How are you now?'* she asked. *'I'm fine dear.'* replied Mom with a smile. *' You know something ma! Your son is recruiting a person to help you.'* said Anamika. *'Yes. He was saying something about interviews.'* replied Mom with a giggle. *'Yes'* chuckled Anamika. *'He is crazy'* said Mom. *'He is crazy but sweet. He is very loving and caring.'* said Anamika with a smile. *'Definitely'* replied Mom. *'He is the best thing happened in my life.'* said Anamika. Mom hugged and gave her bunch of kisses.

Vedha entered the room, *'Ana! Come fast. That lady has arrived . We've to interview her.'* said Vedha. Anamika giggled and followed him. *'Please be seated ma'am'* said Anamika. The lady s at in the couch. *'We saw your profile. We think you're perfect and satisfying our expectations.'* said Vedha. *'More than a helper and nurse. We want a you as a part of our family.'* said Anamika with a smile. *'Sure ma'am. I love to be a part of this beautiful family.'* replied the lady. *'Ana! Take her to Mom.'* said Vedha. *'Okay Bhaiya!... Ma'am please come with me.'* said Anamika and took the lady to Mom's room. Anamika and the lady went to Mom, Mom welcomed her with a smile. *'Ma! She is the one who is gonna help you.'* said Anamika. *'Hello dear. What is your name?'* asked Mom. *'Nancy'* replied the lady. Mom smiled, *'No need to panic. You can be comfortable with us. I want you as a companion.'* said Mom with a smile. *'Sure ma'am.'* replied the lady. *' My son is a busy cop. And my daughter is assisting him in his official cases. She is a criminologist. I'm lonely in this house. I feel bored often.'* said Mom. *'Hereafter, We'll have good time ma'am.'* replied N ancy. *'First of all don't call me ma'am. Call me Ma.'* said Mom with a smile. Nancy smiled. *'Thank you for being here Nancy. You can start your work from tomorrow.'* said Vedha. *'Thank you sir'* said Nancy and left from their home.

Three days passes, it was Anamika's convocation day. Anamika opened her mobile phone. She was astounded when she saw the event posters. *'Bhaiya!'* she screamed in happiness. She ran to her brother and hugged him. ' *You're the chief guest for my ceremony.*' she yelled in happiness. *'Yes. I was invited before a week. I got the official confirmation before two days. I want to surprise you, that's why I did not r eveal it to you sweetheart.*' said Vedha. Anamika smiled, ' *I'm super excited.*' replied Anamika. *'Get ready fast. Let's leave to your college.*' said Vedha. *'I feel proud to come along with the chief guest.*' said Anamika. Vedha smiled. Anamika left to her room and got ready. *'I'm ready*' yelled Anamika and came with a bang. Vedha smiled, *'Come! Get into the car.*' he said. Anamika followed and they left to to her college, *'Bhaiya! I'm getting down here. I'll join my friends. You can go through the Gate A.*' said Anamika. *'Okay Ana! Be safe!* ' replied Vedha and drove to Gate A. Anamika walked in the lane which headed to the back gate of her college.

She walked few steps. A black jeep followed her and stopped near her. Anamika jerked, a man opened and came out of the jeep. He was dressed in black and he wore a mask to hide his face. Anamika's heart beat fast, she tried to dial in her phone. The man pulled her she tried to obstruct him. The man closed her face with a towel which contained a kind of sedative drugs. That moment, Anamika fainted. The man carried her and placed her in his jeep and drove away from the spot. Anamika's kidnap was not noticed by anyone.

After few hours the ceremony was started, Vedha was on the stage as the chief guest. After consecutive speeches from the college board members and chief guests, the ceremony pursued by calling the graduates on the stage and honouring them. Vedha's eyes searched for Anamika. The head of the department called out the names of the students and the students climbed on the stage. After few moments, Anamika's name was called. The head called her name few more times. But she did not turn up. Vedha's face turned tensed. Then the head continued calling the remaining students names. Vedha got panicked and searched for Anamika.

Later the ceremony ended, Vedha went to the head of the department, *'What happened to Anamika?'* asked Vedha. *'Hello sir. She is absent for the ceremony today.'* replied the head. *'No ma'am. I was the one who dropped her here.'* said Vedha. *'What?'* replied the head in shock. *'I'm her legal guardian.'* said Vedha. *'Then how she wa s not available today?'* asked the head. *'I really don't know ma'am. Please help me in finding her.'* said Vedha. *'Okay sir. Let's inform about this to the principal.'* said the head and took him to the principal's cabin. They explained about Anamika's disappearance. The principal took them to the surveillance room. They checked the footages and found that Anamika did not enter the college. *'She did not even enter college.'* said Vedha. *'When did you see her at last?'* asked the principal. *'I left her near the back gate. Then I came to the ceremony '* replied Vedha. *' Okay sir... Ma'am, kindly checkout with her classmates, ask whether they saw her today'* said the principal. *'Sure sir'* replied the head and took Vedha to Anamika's classroom. *' Did anyone see Anamika today?'* asked the head. *'No ma'am'* yelled the students. *'Not only in the ceremony, I'm asking even out of the campus.'* asked the head. *'No ma'am she was absent to the ceremony also and we did not find her anywhere.'* replied the students. *'No one noticed her sir. I think she disappeared at out of the campus.'* said the head. *'Yes ma'am. I'll find out. Thank you'* replied Vedha and left from the college. He went to the spot where he left Anamika. Vedha walked on the muddy road, after few steps. He noticed the trials of a drag in a spot. He also found Anamika's broken anklet. This gave him a clear vision that Anamika was kidnapped.

Meanwhile, the man took Anamika to his basement. He tied her legs and hands to the pillars with metallic chains. Anamika fell on the floor and she was out of conscious. The man locked her in that room and left out.

After an hour, the man came back to Anamika and sprinkled water on her face. *'Uh... Why did you bring me here? Who are you?'* y elled Anamika. The man remained silent. He placed the food items and a pack ag ed water bottle near here. *'Answer me! Who're you?'* yelled

Anamika. The man left the room and locked her again. Anamika pulled her hands and legs violently and screamed to let her out. The man did not respond her. She noticed the light from bottom gap of her door and she also heard some sounds from the front room. *'You will pay for this, I'm sure... Let me out'* she screamed. The man banged her door, *'Ushhh'* he replied. *'Who are you?'* she screamed again. The man banged again. After few moments, she pulled the food package near her. She opened the package and saw Kulcha Parathas and Kadai gravy. Her mind connected and took her to the thoughts of her first date. She remembered her outing with Rudra where they left to marine drive and had dinner together. That day, Anamika said Kulcha Paratha is her favourite food. *"Is he Rudra"* she thought.

After sometime, the man came back to the room to check her. He saw the uneaten food packages. Anamika stared at him, *'Aren't you hungry?'* asked the man. Anamika stayed silent. T he man saw her, *'Remove your mask'* said Anamika. The man tried to move away. Anamika held the man and pulled out his mask. The man stumbled. Anamika saw his face and called *'Rudra'* . Rudra pushed her away, *'Yes. I am'* he yelled. Anamika's eyes dropped out tears. *'You know, you was the first lady who I loved, who I cared. You're the last lady too. I know that police dog smelled right, Vedha!... your beloved brother.'* he said with a laugh and lit his cigarette. Anamika's heart beat fast. *'How Anamika? He reached to my Villa, then to Swarga charity and to my first charity. He has a great sense of smell'* he said and laughed continously.

Rudra sat down, *'Do you remember what you promised me?... You said that you'll be with me forever. So, you should keep that promise. You should not leave me.'* he said and came close to her. Anamika's heart beat fast, she moved back. *'Don't scream. Don't skip your meal. And don't ever think of escaping from here'* he said with a pat on her cheeks. He smiled and left the room and locked her. Anamika sobbed, *'Rudra! Rudra!'* she called. Rudra opened the door and asked, *'Yes sweetheart!'. 'Did you kill them?'* he asked. *'Oh my brave criminologist sweety!'* he said, he pulled the chair and sat near her. *'Don't you speak about us? About reconstructing our love!'* he asked with a smile. Anamika stared. *'Shall I suggest you some blissful topics? You are clinging on the crimes sweetheart!'* said Rudra and twirled her hair. Anamika remained silent. *'Hey honey! You know how much I missed you?* asked Rudra. *'I was praying that you should not be that murderer.'* she said with smile, her eyes rolled out tears.

Rudra closed his eyes and sighed, *'You're just clinging to the crime. It's not your mistake, you a r e a criminologist. Isn't it funny that a psycho fell in love with a criminologist?'* asked Rudra with a chuckle. Anamika looked at his eyes. *'Alan behave yourself. Don't do your mischief here. Stay in the front room.'* yelled Rudra seeing the door. Anamika turned, there was no one standing there. *'To whom are you speaking?'* asked Anamika. *'Uhhhh..... You're such a question box'* yelled Rudra angrily. *'You're not here to question me and I'm not here to answer you.'* he raged. He went out and locked the door with a bang. That night, Rudra came back with food. He placed near her, *'How many days can you survive without having food?'* asked Rudra with a smile. Anamika remained silent. Rudra took her phone from his pocket, *'You have a cute phone. Come let's take a selfie. '* he said and clicked a photograph with her. *'Such a cute family. But let's have our click as your wallpaper.'* he said and changed the clicked selfie as her wallpaper. *'I can't return your phone. I won't let you to call your brother.'* he said and smirked. Anamika kept her hands on her head and sighed. *' You should never show your anger to your food. This was advised by you. So please have the food '* said Rudra. *'I'll starve and die. Leave me alone.'* she cried. *'What is your problem? You love me. I love you. I want to make love with you.'* he said. She closed her eyes. *'Do you love me still?'* he asked. Anamika remained silent and stared at him. *' I love you still. I will love you till my last breathe, a s I promised.'* he said and left the room. Then, he went out through the main entrance.

Anamika heard the sound of his jeep and she found that he left the basement. She thought to break her chains. She saw a stone in the corner of her room. She tried herself and moved to the corner. She picked the stone, rubbed forcibly on the floor and made it sharp. She hit on the chains which were tied to her legs and arms. After some hits, she was able to break the chains. She stood and peeped out to check if someone was there. The whole basement was silent. She ambled to the front room. The room had a small television, a dinning table and four chairs at the corner of the room. Then she walked to the kitchen. She opened the freezer, she found a package of human parts. Anamika was petrified and her heart beat fast. She left the place fast. She walked to the other room and tried to open, but it was locked. After few seconds, she heard terrific yaps at her back. She turned, it was Rudra's Rottweiler. The dog looked at her furiously, his sharp teeth were out and his mouth was watering. Anamika moved a step back, the dogs barked loudly and bit her ferociously. Anamika groaned in pain, she took a pipe which was lying aside and hit the dog with the pipe. She went back to her room and locked herself. The dog yapped ferociously and banged on the door. She sobbed in pain, her leg was bleeding.

After few hours, Rudra returned. *'Ryan Stay! Stay!'* he yelled. The dog calmed, he tied the dog to the pillar. He entered in her room and checked on Anamika. He noticed that she was lying in pain. He also noticed her chains were broken. Then, he went to the nearby pharmacy and bought medicines. *'Anamika get up!'* he called.

Anamika raised and sat. Rudra cleaned her wound and applied some ointment. He gave her an injection and tablets. *'Rudra!'* she called. He left the room without any reply. After few moments, she heard moans and cries of the dog. She peeped out, Rudra was savagely hitting the dog. The dog bled and fell down in pain. Anamika frightened, ' *Oh my god! He is really horrendous."* she thought to herself. Rudra was sweating and his eyes were fierce, his face was red in rage. He took long breathes and gasped continuously. He sat on the chair and closed his eyes. He sat in the same position for a long time. Anamika stared at him and was totally scared and perplexed looking at his actions. She saw the Rottweiler, it looked dog-tired. After sometime, Rudra got up and gave first aid to the dog. He sat near the dog, *'Oh my Ryan! I've said several times to behave yourself. You know that I can't control my emotions. Why should you become a prey of my anger? You're the only one, I have.....'* cried Rudra. He was continuously ranting to the dog.

His actions were totally stunned Anamika. She sat silently and watched his actions. Rudra went to the kitchen and took the meat. She mixed the meat in the rice and served to the dog. The dog was unable to raise. Rudra fed the dog, he was looking sad and emotional. *'Sorry Ryan!'* he cried, he hugged and kissed the dog. Rudra pampered and calmed the dog. The dog ate the food and fell asleep. Rudra patted the dog softly.

After few moments, Rudra returned to Anamika, he lifted her and walked ahead. *'What are you doing, Rudra?'* she yelled. He took the key and opened the locked room. He dropped her down hardly and locked the door. *'Ouch!'* she yelled in pain. The room was so dark, Anamika spooked. After few moments, Rudra returned to the room and turned on the lights. Anamika was shocked, the walls of the room had blood stains. The room had a long table and a tall cupboard. The room looked like a butcher's stall. Rudra had a heavy machete in his hand, *'Gonna slay me?'* asked Anamika. He smirked, *'Not so cruel!'* he replied.

8.3 The Escape

Rudra opened the cupboard and took a man's body. Anamika's eyes widened in shock. He placed the man's body on the long table. He tied the man to the table with leather belts. He took a bucket of water and poured on his face. The man woke up with a sigh. Rudra looked furious, *'Welcome back to your reality '* he yelled. *'Rudra leave me! Please! I'll give you whatever you want. I will do whatever you say. Please leave me!'* begged the man. *'Oh! You mean a b ribe?'*

laughed Rudra. The man cried in fear. *'I hate bribes my dear friend. Because I don't even know what I want.'* he replied and laughed continuously. Rudra's evil laughs scared Anamika. He took a heavy hammer in his hands, *'Lets play a game. I will ask you few questions. For each correct answer, I will remove one belt. For a wrong answer, I will give you a hammer shot.'* he said giggling. The man shivered in fear. *'Did you feel pity on the little girl whom you raped and murdered?'* asked Rudra. The man startled, *'Rudra please leave me!'* he cried. *'Wrong answer'* roared Rudra and stroke the hammer on his chest. The man groaned in pain. He stroked continuously and b lood s cattered on all sides. She screamed in fright. *'I will not leave him father! I'll never listen to you on this'* he yelle d. Rudra was hallucinating. Rudra took the machete violently and stabbed all over his body. Then he amputated the man's right arm, *'This is the bloody hand which made the molest'* he yelled and threw the hand. The amputated hand flew and fell on the floor. Anamika fainted in fear.

Later, Rudra packed the corpse of the man and took it in his jeep. He headed to the nearby village and threw the corpse in the large sew. After few hours, he returned back to the basement.

Anamika opened her eyes, Rudra threw a bag to her. She opened the bag, it had new clothes. *'Rudra, I want to use restroom'* she said. He showed the way.

She went to the restroom, refreshed herself and changed her clothes. Rudra cleaned the blood in the long table. He took the amputated arm and started to removed the fleshes of the arm. She came out from the restroom, she trembled by see ing Rudra's behaviour. He put the bone in a wooden casket. Anamika peeped, she was shocked to see many bones in the casket. S he screamed in fright. He stared at her anxiously. *'Rudra, leave this. I'll take you to a doctor. Come out of this and start a new life.'* she cried. Rudra stared. *'I will say my brother to help you. You're not a person to be punished.'* she cried. *'Who are you to order me to start a new life?'*

he yelled in rage.   Anamika cried silently. *'They're sinners. They've no place to live on this earth.'* he yelled. *'Who are you to punish them?'* Anamika yelled furiously. *'I'm born to kill these molesters. I'm the one.'* he yelled and held Anamika's hair violently. *'If you're gonna kill all men who molests. No man can live on this earth. Each and every girl on this earth has gone through such molests at some point of their life.'* she yelled in pain. He pushed her violently, *'Not all men are like this. You've a dirty perspective.'* replied Rudra furiously and pushed her furiously.

Rudra became violent, he kept his hands on his head and screamed violently. He banged his hands on the wall. S he was shocked. Rudra fainted at that moment. *'Rudra! Rudra!'* she called. Then she ran to the front room and got a bottle of water. She sprinkled the water on his face. Rudra opened his eyes, *'Leave me alone! Go back to your room.'* he said in low tone. *'I'm sorry.'* she replied. *'Please go back to your room. I want to be alone.'* he said. She went back to her room.

After an hour, Anamika heard wail ing sounds. She walked back to the room where Rudra was there. He was sobbing, *'What happened to you?'* she asked. *'Don't worry Mom. I will not leave him.'* he babbled and wiped the floor with a cloth. *'Rudra!'* she called. H e rolled on the floor and cried hardly. She sat near him and held him, *'Calm down! Calm down!'* she said and fondled his head softly. Suddenly, he raised up and yelled, he took the machete and stroked in air. *'Dare to touch my Mom now'* he yelled and ran around the room. Anamika's heart got heavy, her eyes dropped tears. Rudra's neck was cut by his own machete while running around. She yelled, *'Rudra! Be safe. Stay calm'.* Rudra stopped, blood oozed from his neck. Anam ika rushed to him, and held his neck with her shawl. *'No Mom! I'm not hurt. I'm going to slay them. I won't let them to touch you. '* he said furiously. She hugged and calmed him. After some moments, *'Anamika! What a re you doing?'* he asked. Anamika smiled.

Rudra was bleeding continuously, his shirt was wet in blood. *'You're hurt '* she said. *'How this happened?'* he asked by seeing his bleeding neck. She remained silent. *'I'll apply medicine now'* he said and left to the front room. He took the first aid box. *'I will help you'* s he s aid. She cleaned the wound and applied the ointment. And s he covered the wound with a bandage. *'Thank you'* said Rudra with a smile. Anamika smiled, *'You'll be better if you sleep for a while'* she said. Rudra smiled and walked to the room. He lied on the floor. Rudra was murmuring something, *'Rudra! Can you come to my room?'* she asked. Rudra lied without responding. Anamika pulled and raised him. She took him out from that room and took him to her room. *'You did not have these food.'* he said by seeing the uneaten food packages. Anamika smiled. *'Shall we have food together?'* he asked. Anamika agreed and nodded her head. *' But the food has turned cold '* he said. *'I will reheat it.'* she said and took the food package to the kitchen. *'Anamika! Throw away the food which I bought morning. Heat the new one alone.'* he said. He pulled and sat on a chair in the front room. Rudra switched on the television and turned on to a news channel.

The channel displayed Anamika's photo and the news reader read *"20 year old criminology student kidnapped."*, Anamika came to the front room and peered to the television. *'You're a celebrity now'* said Rudra with a giggle. *'It is gonna be a big issue. My brother will surely trace us.'* she said. *'Don't worry, no one can trace us.'* he said. She left to the kitchen silently. She reheated the food and placed on the dinning. *'Hey my lady!'* yelled Rudra in happiness. Both had the food together, *'This scenario takes me back to our first dine together. Do you remember Zakir's restaurant?'* he asked enthusiastically. *'Yes. I do remember'* replied Anamika without any expression. *'Do you want to be with your family?'* he asked. Anamika continued to have the food without any reply. Rudra held her hand, *'Answer me! Don't you wish to be with me?'* he yelled. Anamika stared at him. Rudra pushed his plate and left the dine. She cleaned the table and swept all the rooms expect the room where the murder was done.

Rudra felt bloomed. He came and hugged her, *'Will you be with me?'* he asked. *'I will be with you. But you should accept my demands.'* she said. Rudra laughed hardly. *'I'm talking seriously.'* she said. *'Alright madam! Go ahead with your demands.'* he said. *'I want you to come with me and take your treatment. I know you're suffering from Schizophrenia. You definitely need some medication s '* she said. *'You're the one who know everything about me'* he said. He grabbed her tightly and kissed her. Anamika smiled. *' It is 3 am now, we should take a sleep.'* he said. *'Yes'* she replied.

Rudra took the mattress and placed in her room. *' Have good sleep'* he said and walked to the other room, *'Rudra! Don't go there. I'm afraid to sleep alone.'* she said. Anamika thought his behaviours are changing and weird when he is in that room. He nodded his head and took a blanket and placed in her room. She peeped, *'You can sleep on the mattress. I will sleep on the blanket.'* he said with a smile. He switched off the lights and lit a single lamp in their room. *'Are you comfortable in sleeping o n the blanket ?'* she asked. Rudra laughed, *'Excuse me madam! I've kidnapped you. Don't forget that'* he said. Anamika giggled. After few minutes of silence, *'It has been 20 years since sleeping with a person.'* he said. *'Can't get you'* she replied. *'I slept with my Mom 20 years back. After that, I was sleeping alone these years.'* he said with a smile. Anamika smiled.

After few moments, Anamika heard snores from Rudra, Anamika confirmed that h e was asleep. She raised and ambled silently. Sh e went to the front room and searched for her mobile. She found her mobile in the shelf, she took and switched it on. She found that the SIM was not in the phone. Then, s he heard coughing sound from her room so she rushed back to her room. Anamika felt restless that night, she was sleepless. The morning sun rose, *'Good morning sweetheart'* said Rudra. She smiled. He saw the clock, *'It is 7 am. I will go and get some food for us.'* he said. She was unable to get up, her leg was swollen. *'I'm unable to raise up'* she groaned in pain. Rudra saw her leg, *'Oh my god!'* he yelled. Anamika held her legs and cried in pain. *' We should definitely consult a doctor.'* he said. *' Yeah. I can't bear the pain.'* she said. Rudra raised her, *'Get ready. We'll leave to hospital now.'* he said. Anamika got freshened up and they left to the nearby hospital.

Anamika was treated for dog bites and bruises. Rudra went to the pharmacy to buy medicines. She walked to the reception, *'I want to make a call. Can you give your phone'* she asked. *'Sure ma'am '* said the receptionist and gave her mobile phone. Anamika dialled to Vedha, after few rings, he picked up the call, *'Bhaiya! I'm Anamika. I'm safe. Come soon to Richard hospital.'* she said in rush. *'Ana! How are you?'* he stammered in shock. *'I'm fine. Come as soon as possible.'* she said and ended the call. She walked back to her ward and sat on her bed. *'Where did you go?'* asked the nurse. *'I went to have some water.'* replied Anamika. *'Okay ma'am. Don't move anywhere. Now I'm going to put a dropper for you.'* she said. *'Okay sister'* replied Anamika. After few minutes, Rudra came to her ward. *'How are you now?'* he asked. *'Better'* replied Anamika with a smile. *'I've got medicines for you as per the prescription.'* he said with a smile. *'Okay'* replied Anamika.

After an hour, Anamika's treatment was over and she was discharged. Vedha rushed to the hospital, at that moment, Anamika and Rudra walked out from the hospital. Vedha was tensed to see Anamika wounded, then he saw Rudra's face for first time. His heart was filled with vengeance and his eyes were red in rage. Anamika searched around for Vedha but she didn't notice him. Anamika and Rudra got in the car and left from the hospital. Vedha followed them. They headed to the basement, Vedha stopped at the edge of the road and noticed the m. After few minutes, Vedha entered into the basement silently, he hid himself behind a tree. He peeped inside through a window. Anamika was sitting in a room and Rudra was sitting before the television. Vedha removed his jacket and took out his gun, he ambled inside. He stood behind Rudra and put his jacket on his head. Rudra yelled, Vedha pulled him down and held him with his knees. He tied his hands backward with his jacket. Rudra opposed and resisted him. Anamika rushed to the front room.

'*Bhaiya!*' she yelled. Rudra yelled and tried to relive from his knock. Vedha hit him continuously with his gun. Rudra's face oozed out blood, his vision blurred and he fainted. '*Why did you hit him like this?*' cried Anamika. Rudra gave a perplexed look. '*We ha ve no time. We should take him under our control before he wakes up.*' said Rudra. '*Bhaiya! Listen to me*' she replied. 'Hurry up Ana!' said Vedha and lifted Rudra. '*Get into the car*' he yelled. Vedha and Anamika locked the basement, they took Rudra in their car and left from there.

Chapter-9

9.1 The Tactic Attack

' *How are you Anamika?*' asked Vedha. Anamika remained silent. Vedha stared, *'Are you alright?'* he asked again and shook her shoulders. *'Bhaiya! Why did you hit him? He is really helpless. He needs medical help. He is not a person to be punished.'* whined Anamika. *'Are you out of your senses?'* yelled Vedha. *'Bhaiya! Listen to me. His past life, his mental disorder and his lonely life are the reasons of his murders. I was with him for a day. His behaviour made my heart heavy. After showing some kindness, he behaved totally different. All he needs is some love and kindness. Please understand!'* she cried.

Rudra slowed downed the car. He closed his eyes and lied on the steering. V edha sighed, *'Do you realise what are you speaking?'* he yelled. *'Yes. I do'* he replied. *'What we're doing is not ethic. We should've informed about him to our senior officials.'* he said. *'No. It won't be fair. He should be given a proper medical support.'* she ranted. Vedha gave a hard hit, *'Ouch!'* yelled Anamika. *'If you have been with him for a day, you'll understand.'* she cried. *'I don't want to hear any thing from you. Please stop your senseless rants.'* he yelled in anger.

Anamika wiped her tears. Vedha headed to their home, *'Get down!'* he yelled. Anamika stepped out from the car, Mom rushed out the home and hugged Anamika, *'Where did you go these days my dear? Who kidnapped you?'* she cried. Anamika cried silently, *'Don't worry Mom. I'm fine.'* she replied. *'Ma! Take her inside. Be safe. I'll be back in some time.'* he said. *'Where are you going? I'll also come with you.'* said Anamika. Rudra stared angrily and left from there. *'What happened to him?'* asked Mom. *'I don't know Mom'* replied Anamika. *'Leave him. What happened to you? Who did this? Say me.'* asked Mom. Anamika walked with strain, *'Hey! What happened to your leg?'* yelled Mom. *'I was bitten by a dog.'* replied Anamika. *'Oh my god! How much suffering for you.'* cried Mom. *'Don't worry ma! I will be fine.'* replied Anamika. *'I'm saying from my heart. The person who kidnapped will pay for this. His hell days are coming near.'* said Mom. *'Ma! Don't say like this.'* cried Anamika and returned back to her room. Mom was perplexed by her reply. Anamika went to her room and lied on her bed, she sobbed in dismay. Mom entered to her room. Anamika wiped her tears.

Mom sat on her bed, *'I'm clueless about your behaviour. Say me what happened? Who is he?'* asked Mom. *'Ma! I don't whether I'm right or not. But I believe that Rudra is not a person who should be punished.'* cried Anamika. *'Rudra?'* she replied in shock. *' Yes ma! His childhood was not smooth, it was fully filled with dark incidents. His Mom was raped by many men. S he died in front of him. He ran away from his home at a very young age. He was adopted by a charity. He lived rest of his life alone. These all lead him to a mental disorder called Schizophrenia. I saw his behaviour while attacking a men, he was unable to control himself. He screamed and rolled all over the floor. After knowing I was bitten, h e beat his dog brutally . But when I showed him some kindness, he was totally a different person. He turned into the beautiful person whom I loved the most.'* said Anamika and the tears flowed from her eyes. *'What are you saying?'* asked Mom in shock. *'Yes ma. I fell in love with him without knowing this. He has a beautiful heart, he helped the people in the charity. He was very caring and lovable. My days turned into heaven after loving him. But after knowing all this, it is a hell now.'* she cried. *'I've no words to say.'* replied Mom. Anamika sobbed heavily, her eyes turned red and her face turned pale. *'Don't cry my dear. We'll speak to Vedha about this.'* consoled Mom. *'No ma! I said this to Bhaiya. He scolded me... Rudra should not be punished. He is poor and helpless.'* cried Anamika. *'Trust my words. I will speak to Vedha'* said Mom.

Anamika wiped her tears. *'You should not cry. Take rest for a while.'* said Mom. Mom called Vedha over phone. He did not pick her call. She tried again several times, but he did not respond to any of her calls. *'He is not picking the calls'* said Mom. *'What shall we do now?'* asked Anamika. *'Let's call to his colleague and check.'* said Mom. *'Okay ma!'* replied Anamika and dialled the inspector's phone number. *'Hello ma'am'* said the inspector over the call. *'I'm Anamika. Where is Bhaiya?'* she asked. *'Ma'am he is off on duty today. He did not come to the station.'* informed the inspector. *'Okay sir. If he comes there let me know'* replied Anamika. *'Sure ma'am'* replied the inspector and ended the call. *'Bhaiya did not leave to the station. He has gone somewhere else.'* said Anamika. *'Don't think too much. He should come here only at the end of the day.'* said Mom. Anamika turned and sat with a groan. *'Take rest dear, sleep for a while.'* said Mom. Anamika flattened on the bed and closed her eyes. Mom went to the kitchen and boiled some milk for her. She returned back to her room with a glass of milk, *'Dear, have this milk.'* said Mom. Anamika got the milk and drank. Mom patted her head. *'Everything is gonna be fine.'* she said with a smile. Anamika smiled.

That night, it was around eleven. V edha came back home and w alked directly to the basement. Mom was cleaning the kitchen, Anamika was sitting in the dinning chair tiredly. Mom heard some sounds from the basement, *'Did you hear some sound s from the backyard ?'* asked Mom. *'No ma. Wait lemme check'* said Anamika. A nd she stepped out from the house and walked to the backyard. *'Yes ma. Someone is there in the basement'* yelled Anamika. *'Wait. Don't go alone'* yelled Mom and rushed to her. Both the ladies walked to the basement. Anamika opened the basement door forcibly, *'Vedha!'* yelled Mom.

Vedha was tying Rudra with a rope in a wooden chair. Rudra was in a drowsy state, he was brutally injured and his dress was torn. Anamika was shocked, *'What have you done to him ?'* she screamed and walked to Rudra. Vedha pushed her away. *'What is this Vedha?'* asked Mom. *'You both leave from here. I'm a cop. I know how to handle this'* said Vedha furiously. *'Rudra!'* cried Anamika. *'Behave like a human, Vedha!. You've hit him hard and he is bleeding.. . Understand! He is not a normal man. He is mentally unstable'* said Mom and tried to remove the rope, Vedha hindered her. *'Ana! Go and get some water.'* said Mom. *'What a re you doing ma?'* yelled Vedha. Anamika ran to the kitchen and got a jug of water. Mom pushed Vedha, she took some water in her palms and sprinkled in Rudra's face. Anamika went to him, *'Rudra! Rudra!'* she called and tapped on his cheeks. Rudra slowly opened his eyes. Mom went in and got the first aid kit. Vedha sighed, *'I made a blunder by bringing him here'* he yelled. Rudra murmured something and looked around. His eyes turned to Anamika. Rudra stared at her. *'Rudra!'* called Anamika and ran to him. He remained silent, his eyes were empty and still. *'Hey Betta! Don't get panicked. What is happening to you?'* asked Mom. Vedha raised his eyebrow, *'Betta? You're calling him as your son'* he yelled in anger. *'Please stay quite .'* said Mom. Rudra's eyes dropped down tears. *'Don't cry dear'* said Mom and wiped his tears. Rudra closed his eyes slowly and fainted at that moment. *'Oh my god!'* yelled Anamika. *'I think we should take him to the hospital.'* said Mom. *'No way. Do you have any sense? I'm in investigation. I want to enquire him and produce him to the crime department soon.'* yelled Vedha. *'He is wounded. He needs some treatment'* said Mom. *'He is a criminal ma. Have that in your mind'* yelled Vedha. *'What you are doing is also against the law.'* yelled Anamika furiously.

Vedha stared at her angrily. Mom again sprinkled some water on his face. Rudra woke up and hugged her. Mom smiled and tapped on his back. Vedha and Anamika got shocked by seeing this scene. Mom gave him first aid. *'Get up from here.'* said Mom and took him inside their home. Anamika giggled at Vedha. *'You're laughing at me.'* yelled Vedha and chased her. Anamika ran in. Mom made Rudra to sit in the dine and served him some food. Rudra's face looked weary. He moved his hands to the food but he was unable to pick a bite. Mom took a piece from the chapati and dipped it in the sabji, she moved her hand to his mouth. Rudra looked at her. *'Have a bite'* said Mom with a smile. Rudra's eyes dropped out tears. Mom fed him and pampered him. Anamika was shocked. *'I'm sorry Rudra. I did not expect this is gonna happen'* pleaded Anamika. Rudra remained silent and stared at Mom. Anamika waved her hand at him. Rudra pushed her hand and was looking at Mom. Vedha was sitting on the couch, his eyes were closed and his hands were on his head. Mom took the pain-killers and walked to Rudra, *'Have these tablets and sleep well.'* said Mom with a smile. Rudra dropped the tablets in his mouth and gulped it with some water. *'You should never put the tablets together. Have each one at a time'* she said with a smile. Rudra smiled. Vedha peeped at them in shock. Anamika giggled. Mom took him to the bed room and made him to lie. She sat near him and comforted him. After some moments, Rudra fell in deep sleep.

Mom closed the door and came out. Vedha looked at her, *'Are you out of your mind?'* he asked. *'The moment when I saw him, I felt really pity. My heart said to calm him. '* said Mom. Vedha was shocked. Mom sat near Vedha in the couch. *'See Vedha, he is younger than you. His pa st is a woe. He is mentally unstable. He should be taken to rehabilitation.'* said Mom softly. *'Ma! You've not seen the victim's body. His attacks are brutal. He is really dangerous.'* replied Vedha. Mom nodded her head. *'He is a serial killer. One month ago, whole country was on panic after hearing his attacks. I feel guilty. What I'm doing is against the laws.'* he said in worry. *'Vedha, stay calm. Don't worry. Think what to be done next!'* said Mom. *'I've decided. I'm going to produce him with all my investigation and evidences to the higher officials.'* said Vedha. *' A lright! Now you go and sleep.'* said Mom. *'How can I sleep? We're having a killer in our house.'* replied Vedha. Mom smiled and held his hand. *'You go and sleep ma. Be with Anamika.'* said Vedha. *'Okay! I'm leaving. Goodnight!'* said Mom and left to her room.

Vedha went to the study room and started reading his case files. He was unable to concentrate. He closed his eyes and rested backwards on his chair. His mind was disturbed and flooded with random thoughts. He opened the door of the room where Rudra was sleeping, Vedha entered the room silently and checked him. Rudra was sleeping. He locked back the door and left to the room where Anamika and Mom was there. They were also sleeping. Vedha walked to the dining hall and drank some water from the jug. His phone rang, it was a call from Viswa. Vedha walked to the terrace and started speaking to him. Meanwhile, Rudra got up from his room. He was not really asleep, he pretended. He was actually snooping on Vedha. He ambled to the study room and hunted for something. He noticed a half closed drawer. He opened it and found a pistol with a silencer. Rudra smirked. He took the pistol and ambled to the terrace.

Vedha was standing near the wall and was on his call. Rudra took the iron rod which was lying on the floor and ambled behind Vedha. He gave a hard hit on his head. Vedha groaned in pain. Rudra gave several hard strikes on his head. Vedha collapsed down. Rudra took the pistol out, *'Good Bye my brother'* he e xclaimed and shot on his left chest. Rudra jumped to a window slab from the terrace and escaped from their home. Vedha was was brutally injured and he collapsed on the spot.

Meantime, Anamika was restless. She was unable to sleep. Her bruise in the leg caused severe pain. She was rolling on the bed. *'What happened to you my dear?'* asked Mom. *' My wound is aching and itching . I'm unable to sleep '* said Anamika. Mom switched on the lights and saw her. *' Oh god! Shall we go to the hospital?'* asked Mom. *'No ma. I'll manage tonight .'* replied Anamika. *'Wait. I'll get a pain-killer for you.'* said Mom and left the room.

She saw the room where Rudra was sleeping, the door was kept open. She also noticed the messy study room. *'Vedha!'* called Mom. Anamika got up from and bed and walked out of the room, *'Where did they go?... Both, Rudra and Vedha are not here.'* said Mom. *'What?!'* exclaimed Anamika. She looked up at the stairs, *'Ma! The terrace door is open.'* she informed. *'Wait. I'll go and check there.'* said Mom and climbed to the terrace. She was shocked to see Vedha lying in the pool blood. *'Vedha!'* she screamed. *'What happened ma?'* yelled Anamika and strained to climbed the stairs. Anamika's eyes widened in shock, her words faded after seeing her brother's condition. *'Call someone'* yelled Mom. Anamika called to emergency. After few moments, the ambulance arrived to their home. Anamika took the ambulance assistants to the terrace and they shifted Vedha to the ambulance. Mom and Anamika followed them to the hospital. Vedha was taken to the critical care ward and his treatment was started.

Anamika was unable to come out from this shock. *'It was all because of me.'* she cried. *'Why a re you worrying? Nothing will happen to Vedha. I trust him. He is a warrior.'* said Mom and wiped her tears. Doctor came, *'Vedha is objected to severe head injury. And gun shot in his chest is deep... We're trying our best. Trust on god.'* he said. Anamika sobbed. *'Don't put th ese words in to your ears. Relax!'* said Mom. *'You be here. I'll go and call my brother for help.'* said Mom. *'Ma! Please! Don't leave me alone. I'm afraid.'* whined Anamika. Mom looked at her, *' Okay! Lemme call him.'* she said. Mom took her phone and walked away to call. Anamika walked and sat on the bench. She felt heavy and disturbed.

Hours passed, Anamika walked to the nurse who came out of the ICU, *'What is Vedha's condition?'* she asked. *'Doctors are treating him ma'am. Don't worry.'* replied the nurse. That night was a sleepless, tough night for Mom and Anamika. Next day, the sun rose, Mom went to their home to get refreshed. Anamika saw the chief doctor entering into the ICU. After few moments, the doctor returned out. Anamika walked to him, *'Sir, What is the condition of*

Vedha?' she asked. *'He is out of danger. But due to the severe shock on his head, he is in a coma state.'* said the doctor. *'When will he be recovered?'* asked Anamika. *'We can't assure. It may take some hours, days or even months. His recovery is associated with his will power.'* replied the doctor and left from there. Mom returned to the hospital with her brother. Anamika ran to her, *'The chief doctor came now. He said Vedha is out of danger.'* said Anamika.

Mom smiled, she closed her eyes and thanked to god. *'But he said, Vedha is in coma.'* cried Anamika. *'Hey Ana! Vedha will wake up soon . He can't be still for a moment. He wants to do something. He is an active man.'* replied Mom with a bright smile. Anamika smiled. *'You go home, take your bath. Sleep for a while and come back here. You've no rest.'* said Mom. Anamika nodded her head. *'No! You don't go home alone. It's not safe. You better go to my home and take rest.'* said Mom's brother. *'Okay uncle!'* replied Anamika. *'Be safe!'* said the man. Anamika left to his home from the hospital.

Anamika returned back to the hospital at evening. *'Are you relaxed?'* asked Mom. Anamika smiled. *'Did you see Bhaiya?'* asked Anamika. *' Yes dear. I saw him in the visiting hours.'* replied Mom. *' How is he?'* asked Anamika. *'He is injured badly. But don't worry, he'll be fine soon.'* replied Mom with a painful smile. Anamika hugged her. *' I want to ask you something. Have you filed a complaint?'* she asked. *'Yes dear. I informed Viswa. He said us to lodge a robbery complaint. He also promised to find Rudra unofficially.'* said Mom . *'The whole investigation was handled in undercover. That's why he said us to file as a robbery case.'* said Anamika. *'I understand'* replied Mom. *' W e trusted him, but   s ee what he ha s don e to us . He'll sure pay for this.'* cried Anamika. Mom calmed her. *'I want to see Bhaiya!'* said Anamika. *'I don't know whether they'll allow now... Come, let's ask in the nurse station.'* said Mom. Both the ladies walked to the nurse station, *'She is my daughter. She wants to see her brother. She is really worried.'* said Mom. *'Okay ma'am. But she should come out soon. It'll be a problem for us if the chief doctor gets to know.'* replied the nurse. *'Sure dear'* said Mom. *'Okay ma'am. Come with me.'* said the nurse and took Anamika to the ICU. *'Don't cry near him.'* said the nurse with a smile. Anamika walked near Vedha. Her heart got heavy. Vedha was in a terrible condition. His head and chest was injured. He was lying still. Anamika held his hand. *'Bhaiya! I'm Anamika. Get up soon, enough of sleeping. Get up!'* she said. Anamika touched his cheeks, *'Come on! Let's put Rudra behind the bar. He should be punished... Punished severely.'* she said emotionally. Anamika took a stool and sat near him. She lied near his hand. *'I've no one Bhaiya! Get up!'* she said and her eyes rolled tears. Vedha's hand moved slightly. Anamika was shocked. *'Bhaiya! Can you hear me?'* she asked. Vedha breathed heavily. Anamika left from the ICU and rushed to the nurse station. *'Sister! My Bhaiya moved his hand. He is taking long breathes'* yelled Anamika. The nurse got up from her seat, Mom and uncle rushed to her. *'Dear! Don't react too much. It is normal... S peak to him. It will help us, he'll respond soon.'* said the nurse with a smile. Anamika wiped her tears, Mom came and held her shoulders. *'Anamika! Do you believe me?'* asked Mom. Anamika nodded her head. *'Vedha will survive from this. He'll recover soon. Pray to god. Don't cry'* she said with a hug. Anamika smiled.

9.2 The Recovery

Days passed, he was battling in the hospital for a month. Then he was shifted back to home.

Around 4 months passed, The valiant man was lying like a doll in his home. A man was employed to take care of Vedha. Anamika's whole lifestyle was changed totally. She got graduated and she was waiting for her UPSC examination results which was one week away. Mom lived in dismay thinking of her son's condition, but she did not lose her hope.

One day, a girl arrived to their home. Anamika was sitting in the hall before the television. Mom was lying in her room. The girl knocked at the open door. Anamika turned at her, *'Who is this?'* she asked. *'I'm Nihana. I heard about Vedha's condition. May I see him?'* asked the girl. *' Please come in. Be seated. I'll call my Mom'* said Anamika and ran to Mom's Room. The girl sat on the couch. *'Ma! A girl arrived to our home. She is looking pretty. She asked permission to see Bhaiya'* she said rapidly. *'What're you speaking?'* giggled Mom. Anamika chuckled. *'A....girl... came to.. see Vedha'* she said slowly with a wink. *'You crazy girl!'* said Mom and gave a tap on her shoulder. Mom and Anamika walked to the hall. *'Hello dear. Who are you?'* asked Mom. *'I'm Nihana. I want to see Vedha.'* replied the girl. *'Sorry for questioning a lot. It is a murder attempt . So we've to be cautious. Please say us, how you know him.'* said Mom. *'We lov e d each other. He promised me that he'll come to meet me. But he is lying here.'* the girl replied and dropped her tears. Anamika and Mom was shocked. *'I know you'll not believe me. You can ask to Vishwa Bhaiya. He is aware o f our love.'* said Nihana. *'Okay dear. I understand. Please come in'* welcomed Mom. She smiled and wiped her tears with her kerchief. *'Anamika take her in'* said Mom. *'Bhabi!'* she yelled and ran to her. Nihana smiled. Anamika and Nihana left to Vedha's room. Mom went to her room and made a call to Viswa. *'Bhaiya! See who has come'* yelled Anamika. Nihana stood near his bed. She was stunned to see his man in this state. She sobbed.

After some moments, Mom entered the room. Anamika raised her eyebrows and signed *'What?'.* Mom nodded her agreed. *'Don't cry dear. He'll be fine. He is improving.'* said Mom with a smile. Anamika climbed on the bed and sat near Vedha. She bent to his ears, *'You cheat! You did not even say you're in love. How cunning you a re.'* she whispered in his ears and pinched on his arms. Mom saw Anamika, *'Hey Ana! Come out.'* she called. Anamika stared at her and got out from the bed. *'Hey drear. We both will be back in a moment.'* said Mom and took Anamika out. *'Order some special food in online '* said Mom. Anamika giggled, *'Wah.. Wah.. Treat for your daughter-in-law'* she replied. Mom laughed. Anamika took her phone and ordered food in Swiggy.

After few moments, Nihana came out of his room, *'Thank you aunty! I'm leaving.'* she said. *'We've arranged for lunch. Please wait for sometime.'* said Mom. *'Okay aunty'* replied Nihana. *'Bhabi... Come! Be seated'* said Anamika. She held her hand and took her to the couch. The lady trio sat on the couch and started their conversation. *'How do you know Vedha?'* asked Mom. *'We both are friends from our school time.'* replied Nihana. *'When did it grow as love?'* asked Anamika with a funny gesture. *'Ana!... Don't mind her. She is a talkative girl'* said Mom.

The girl bloomed with a smile. *'Bhabi... Say me... Vedha did not even give a single clue on you.'* said Anamika. *'We're in love since past two years.'* replied the girl with a blush. *'Ahan.. Ahan... Don't blush'* she said and held her cheeks. *'What is your profession?'* asked Mom. *'I'm doing my final year college.'* replied the girl. *'What is your stream?'* asked Anamika. *'Masters in mass communication and journalism... MJMC'* she replied. *'Great.. Great'* replied Anamika. *'What about your family?'* asked Mom. *'My dad is a retired colonel. Mom is a home-maker. I have a younger brother, he is doing his high school.'* said Nihana. *'Good'* replied Mom. Anamika's phone rang, it was the Swiggy delivery person. *'Ma! The food has arrived.'* she said and collected the food. *'Come dear. Let's have the food.'* called Mom. Anamika and Nihana was seated on the dine. Mom served them. *'I've no issues on your love. I always live for my children's wish. Their wish is my happiness.'* expressed Mom. *'Mom's heart is purer than gold.'* said Anamika. Nihana smiled. *'Sh e' ll accept an orphan as her daughter. She'll give her food and shelter...'* said Anamika. *'Ana! Stop this. What are you speaking?'* yelled Mom. *'Okay... Okay'* she replied. *'You know something. She'll feed a serial killer.'* said Anamika and laughed hard. *'Oh my god! See this girl's behaviour'* whined Mom. *'Yes Bhabi.. She is not like the typical Mothers.'* said Anamika. *'I know... Vedha has said a lot about you.'* replied Nihana.

'To us, he has never said about you' said Anamika and bobbed her head. Nihana chuckled. They finished their Lunch and Nihana was about to wind up. *'Aunty. Can I come here often? I'm really worried. My heart is always flooded in his thoughts. I'm unable to concentrate on anything. If I come here and see him, it gets warmed.'* she asked. *'Sure dear. You can come here anytime.'* replied Mom with a hug.

Viswa was transferred to Mumbai. His first day of work commenced that day. On afternoon, Anamika went to meet him in the station. She went to his cabin, *'Hey Anamika! Please be seated.'* welcomed Viswa. She looked around, *'Some days, Bhaiya will take me here after my college hours. He used to be working and I'll be sitting on this bench and doing my assignments. Later, we'll return home together after his work. I miss those days.'* said Anamika with a painful smile. *'I understand your pain. You know, I don't have courage to see him.'* he replied in dismay. *'Doctors are saying he is showing some improvements.'* said Anamika. *'Thank God!'* replied Viswa. *'Viswa, You should focus on this case. According to the world, it was a robbery and a murder attempt. But, we know what is the truth. We should trap Rudra as soon as possible.'* said Anamika. *'Hey Anamika! Vedha is my childhood friend. I'm working hard to find him. I'll not leave Rudra, he'll suffer for this. I'm sure.'* said Viswa. *'That's what I want.'* replied Anamika. Viswa smiled. *'Shall we go back and check out in the basement where he kept you kidnapped?'* asked Viswa. *'No. I went there after couple of days. The basement was clean and empty.'* said Anamika. *'You courageous girl! You went there alone?!'* asked Viswa. Anamika took a pack from her bag, *'Yes. I hunted in the whole basement. I found a memory card in a corner of the room. I was unable to access it as was crashed. Then I found this spectacles.'* she said and gave the pack which contained the spectacles and memory card. *'I'll give this to a technical expert and try to retrieve it's content.'* said Viswa. *'Great! And I've found the power of the lens in the spectacles.'* she said and gave the lens's prescription to him. *'You're super-smart, girl!'* said Viswa and shook her hand. *'Thank you Viswa.'* replied Anamika. *'But be careful. You've done a risky* deed.' said Viswa. *'I should do something for my Bhaiya. He is reason for what I'm today.'* said Anamika. *'Of course... And what about your UPSC results?'* asked Viswa. *'5 more days to go'* replied Anamika and her fingers crossed. *' All the best'* replied Viswa. *'Thank you Viswa. I'm leaving.'* said Anamika and returned back to home.

Five days passed, It was the day of UPSC examination result day. Mom went to a temple to offer her prayers. Anamika was nervous, becoming a CID officer is her dream from her childhood. She walked to Vedha's room with her laptop and sat near him. She logged in to the results portal, *'Bhaiya! I'm feeling nervous. The result is going to be out in 15 minutes.'* she said and held his hand. Seconds passed, her heart beat fast. She held his hands tight and closed her eyes. She prayed to god. Mom and Viswa reached home. *'Hey Vedha! Get up! Today is your sister's result.'* exclaimed Viswa. Mom gave her offering and smeared sindoor in her forehead. After few moments, the result was published. Fortunately, Anamika was a topper, she secured 5th rank. *'Hey girl. You made it.'* exclaimed Viswa. Anamika was on her cloud nine. *'Congratulations dear. She spared a whole year for preparation. She did not lose her mind after two attempts... Now she made it... Your hard work paid off.'* said Mom with a hug. *'You're great. I know you've a great future.'* replied Viswa. Seeing this scene, Vedha moved his hands legs, he took long breathes and groaned. *'Vedha!'* yelled Mom and they ran to him. Anamika got on his bed, *'Bhaiya! What is happen ing to you?'* yelled Anamika. *'Ana!'* mumbled Vedha and he tried to hold her hands. *'Oh my god! He has woke up'* replied Viswa. Anamika was stunned, she sat still in astonishment. Mom dropped her happy tears, *'You're alright'* she said and calmed him. She smeared sindoor on his forehead. *'Thank you god!'* prayed Mom. Anamika stared at him, without any reply. *'Now, Anamika has gone into Coma.'* giggled Viswa. Anamika's eyes dropped tears, she hugged Vedha. *'Thank you Bhaiya!'* she cried. Vedha strained and patted her head. Mom called his doctor. Viswa showed Anamika's results to him, *'See your sister's results. She nailed it.'* he said. Vedha smiled at her and tried to speak. *'Don't strain Bhaiya!'* said Anamika.

After an hour, doctor came and checked Vedha. *'It is a miracle and god's grace.'* said the doctor. Everyone there felt happy. *'He should have his physiotherapy sessions regularly. He should have healthy food and take his medicines with out skipping. I'm sure he'll be back to normal within a month.'* said the doctor. *'Thank you doctor.'* replied Anamika. *'I'll share the physiotherapist's contact to you. You can contact him for his sessions.'* he said said. *'Sure sir '* replied Anamika. The doctor gave him medicines and left from their home.

Anamika walked out from the room and called Nihana, *'Hey Bhabi. I'm Anamika. I've a good news for you.'* she said. *' Hey Ana! I know it already. I was about to call you... You secured a high rank in your UPSC results.'* replied Nihana. *'No. That was not the good news which I came to say .'* she replied. *'Then?'* exclaimed Nihana. *'Bhaiya woke up'* she yelled in happiness. *'Oh!'* yelled Nihana back. Both floated in happiness. *'Can you come here?'* asked Anamika. *'Yes. I'm coming soon'* replied Nihana. They ended the call and Anamika returned back to her brother. *'Officer'* mumbled Vedha with a bright smile. Anamika hugged him, *'I love you Bhaiya! I'm really happy today'* she cried in happiness. Vedha strained to moved his hands and wiped her tears. *'I love you too. This is your day. Be happy'* he murmured. *'Bhaiya! One minute. I'll be back... Viswa please take care of him'* said Anamika and she ran to Mom. *'Ma! Nihana is coming.'* informed Anamika. *'Great! She'll be happy to see Vedha'* replied Mom. *'Yes'* she said and ran back to Vedha's room. *'Why are you racing here and there?'* asked Viswa. *'I can't control myself. I feel out of the world.'* said Anamika. *'I know'* replied Viswa with a smile.

After few moments, Nihana came home. Mom took her to Vedha's room. *'Vedha!'* she called. Vedha turned at her, he was shocked. *'Don't forget. You are a brother of a criminologist. You can't escape from me. You've hid about your love to us.'* said Anamika and raised her eyebrow s . Vedha blushed. Nihana giggled, *'She did not find. I surrendered here.'* she replied. Anamika giggled. *'Mr Viswa, come let's move out. Let the couple speak.'* said Anamika. *'Yeah'* replied Viswa. T hen, Anamika and Viswa moved out. *'Do you like my family?'* murmured Vedha. *'This my family too. I love them.'* replied Nihana. Vedha smiled.

The whole family had their lunch and the day was spent well. *'Have you spoken to your family about your love?'* asked Mom. *'Yes aunty. I've s aid to my Mom'* replied Nihana. *'Do inform us when to come to your home. I wish to see Vedha's marriage soon.'* said Mom. *'Sure aunty. I will speak about this to my Mom'* said Nihana. *'Don't mind!, Will your family accept your love? You're Muslim. We're Hindus.'* asked Mom. *'M y Mom is a Hindu and my Dad is a Muslim... Vedha is in good job. I'm also focused on my career. I don't think it'll be an issue.'* replied Nihana with a smile. *'Great. We're living in 21 st century. We should be practical.'* said Mom. Nihana smiled, *' You're right!... Okay aunty. I'm leaving'* she said left home. The day ended unexpectedly.

Few Months passed, Anamika joined in Crime investigation department and her training commenced. She was posted as the sub-inspector and she was working under Viswa. Viswa and Anamika tried to trace Rudra, but they did not even get a single clue on him. The memory card which Anamika found was utter waste, it was crashed completely and they were unable to retrieve. They had no leads on him. There were no similar attacks occurred in the city.

Vedha recovered well. Mom spoke to Nihana's family about their marriage. Both family decided to have their marriage on the following month. That day, Anamika came home late. Vedha was sitting in the veranda. *'Ana! I want to speak something to you'* said Vedha. *'I'll be back, Bhaiya!... Just a minute, I'll get re fresh ed .'* said Anamika. *'Sure dear'* replied Vedha. Anamika took her bath and dressed in her casual clothes. She took a cup of milk and sat near Vedha. *'How was your day Bhaiya?'* she asked. *'It was busy. Whole day went in shopping for the wedding '* he replied. Anamika smiled and had sips of her milk. *'Say me!'* she exclaimed. *'How is your progress in your work?'* he asked. *'I'm doing great Bhaiya!'* she replied with a smile. *'I know. I spoke about you to the commissioner. He said you are doing great. I felt really happy.'* he said. *'Thank you... And when will you be back to work?'* she asked. *'After my marriage... I really feel bored. My mind and heart is in my work.'* he expressed. *'I know'* she replied. *'What is the progress of Rudra's case?'* he asked . *'The department has left the case in pending. Me and Viswa has tried our best to trace him. We did not even get a single clue... Rudra has just vanished.'* she replied . *' He is the most clever and dangerous man, I've ever met.'* he said. *'True!'* she replied. *'You look so tired, let's go for sleep.'* he said. And they left to sleep.

Months passed, Vedha's marriage was over. He married Nihana and he rejoined to his work. He took charge as the deputy superintendent of police. The valiant man proved his efficiency and he became progressive again. Anamika was emerging as a star cop. She mainly worked for women safety. She traced and brought back 5 teen girls who were trafficked to Mumbai. The victims were brutally raped and kidnapped. She nabbed the suspects with help of Vedha and Viswa and produced him to the court. It was the idol hunt of her period which lead her to promotion. She was all set to take charge as the Assistant Superintendent of police.

Chapter-10

10.1 The Ending

It was the ceremony day, Anamika was transferred to Kerala and she was posted as the Assistant Superintendent of Kerala. The whole country appreciated her, she was the talk of the town. In the press meet,   *'Women are valiant. They should have high dreams. I had a dream which fired my soul. I dreamt to become a IPS officer at my age five. That dream carried me to a person who I'm today. I promise to work for the peace and harmony of the country. I promise to work for the empowerment and upliftment of the women. '* she spoke. She walked to her cabin. Later, she got a call from Vedha. *'Congratulations Anamika.'* he wished. *'Thank you Bhaiya'* she replied. *'I've a good news for you.'* said Vedha. *'What?'* she asked eagerly. Nihana grabbed his phone, *'Congratulations dear!'* she said. *'Thank you Bhabi!'* replied Anamika. *' You're going to become an aunt.'* said Nihana happily. *'Wow... It's a great news...'* she yelled in happiness. *'We went to the doctor and got confirmed just now. I felt really happy.'* she said. *'Congrats! We're blessed'* she said. *'Yeah'* replied Nihana. Anamika smiled. *' I'm handing the call to your brother. Bye!'* she said and gave the phone to Vedha. *'Hey daddy'* e xclaimed Anamika. Vedha smiled. *'Congrats Bhaiya!'* she wished. *'Thank you dear'* replied Vedha. *'How is Mom?'* she asked. *'She is sleeping'* replied Vedha. *'I really miss her. She'll be the first person to wish me on my success.'* she replied. *'Yes dear. She is aged and unwell.*

Most of the time, she is sleeping and looking weary.' replied Vedha. *'I understand'* she replied. *'Okay dear. Carry on with your work. We'll speak later.'* he replied and ended the call.

After sometime, the assistant knocked the door, *'Ma'am...May I come in?'* he asked. *'Please come in'* replied Anamika. The man placed a bouquet on her table, *'This is for you ma'am'* said the man. *'Thank you'* replied Anamika. *'May I leave ma'am?'* asked the man. *'Sure'* replied Anamika. The man left from her room. Anamika felt blessed, her dream came true. The nation recognized her as a brave cop.

She saw a n anonymous letter which was inserted in the bouquet. She opened the letter and started to read,

" Dear Anamika,

This letter is from a person to whom you promised to love forever. You're the only person who know me completely. Can you guess me?

I'm doing good. Hope you're also doing great.

You're an inspiration to many youths who dream to achieve. You've no limits, you are like the sky. I admire your bravery. I'm really blessed that I've shared few memorable memories with you. Those memories are sealed in my heart forever. You're the only woman who I love and admire till my last breathe .

I read about your recent encounter, I got to know that you have saved 5 teen girls. I felt really proud of you. The nation needs your service. Let's fight for it, no women should be sexually abused. The world should turn as an abode of heaven. I'm also working on my part for this change. Hope you'll continue your   brave deed. Congratulations and all the best.

Yours Truly,

Your true admirer."

Anamika sensed, she was sur e that it was from Rudra. She got up from her seat and walked to the balcony of her cabin. She looked at the world. The sun shined bright and kissed her forehead. She bloomed in a bright smile.